ANTIQUITY

ANTIQUITY

MICHAEL XAVIER BOGGINS

Antiquity

For information about this title or to order other books and/or electronic media, contact the publisher:

Michael Xavier Boggins
michaelxavierboggins.com
mboggins@cox.net

ISBN: 978-1-7341480-0-8 (paperback)

Printed in the United States of America

Cover and Interior design: 1106 Design

To my daughters Sarah and Abby
for their tireless editing efforts and support

To Kristen for giving Antiquity a good
read and for her encouragement

To the great folks at 1106 Design for shepherding
me through the publishing process

And of course, thanks to the author of all things

CHaPTeR 1

IF I COULD UNRAVEL ANY DAY, it would be that day.

It was cold and windy, and I was standing on roadside, watching my sister Ashley help her friend Stacey. They were moving grocery bags from Stacey's car to Ashley's. Stacey's car had broken down, and she needed rescue. Ashley was parked behind Stacey's car. The wind rose up fiercely when cars sped by, and I turned my back to avoid the worst of it. My teeth chattered, and I clenched my jaw.

They were almost finished; Ashley grabbed the last two bags from Stacey's trunk. She looked my way and smiled. I was five and she seventeen, but I knew that smile—it said "Thank you for not complaining." Funny how a small thing can make you feel—pride warmed me from the inside. Ashley took a step forward, and, suddenly, the world's pace changed; it appeared to be coming to a stop as I watched. I heard the sound of screeching brakes and steel hitting steel. My sister's car seemed to leave the ground as it was propelled forward, crushing Ashley between her car's grill and the back of

Stacey's car. Ashley screamed and screamed until her lungs could no longer muster air. Her screams were replaced with a queer gurgling sound, and blood began to flow from her mouth. Her head dropped and hung at a cockeyed angle, making her look like a doll that had been thrown into a corner. I don't know why, but I remember thinking we were going to be late getting home and mom would be mad.

My sister never came home.

My friends give me shit about being a geek hermit. Maybe they're right; my life is pretty much school and my computer. What's so great about bein' out there? Ashley was just trying to help a friend, and now she's gone.

But you aren't always given a choice.

For me, it started one afternoon. It was a Tuesday afternoon—a clear-blue, breezy autumn afternoon. As I walked home from school, I was planning my evening. I guess it wasn't much of a plan. Get home, homework, and then download software to boost the performance of a new gaming computer I was building.

I was halfway through my homework and was trying to answer yet another civics question that couldn't be found in the textbook or the teacher's less-than-perfect notes. He was asking about a connection between modern civics and Genghis Khan.

I texted my bud, Jason. **WTF? Genghis Khan? What you got? I should ask your sister; she would know. I could ask her to come over to discuss Khan.**

You bastard. My sister is off limits; besides, she wouldn't be caught dead with your sorry ass. No, I got nothin' on Khan.

Jason being no help, I turned to Google. My search netted the usual suspects—Wikipedia, Dictionary.com, and the rest. Another link also appeared—**Khan-forever**. No green check mark; nothing looked legitimate, and a feeling in my gut said, "Move on," but I ignored the internal warning and clicked. Instead of a site centered on the barbarian ruler and his version of civics, I landed on a page crowded with links to apps and games. *A dead end!* I f'n protested, as I had with many dead ends I had encountered before. I started moving my pointer toward the back arrow when a name on the list caught my eye.

Antiquity.

My mouse's pointer slowed and stopped just short of the back arrow. The paragraph below the title suggested one could have a fun-filled adventure seeing how history could be altered by providing "Antiquity" with different scenarios. I figured Antiquity was a lame teaser, but I thought Dad might have fun with it. He was a true history enthusiast. He always had a new book on his nightstand—Lincoln this, Caesar that. *Fine*, I thought, *if it sucks, I'll delete it.* So I double-clicked, and the download started. A progress bar appeared and began its familiar left to right movement. 1%, 2% . . . crap—this is going to take forever. I walked away from my computer and started on my math homework.

I stayed with my algebra for the next forty minutes and didn't think about Antiquity until my PC pinged.

I bumped the mouse. The screen lit, and I entered my Windows password.

Whoa!

I was staring at a screen filled with graphics that were vivid, a melding of art and reality. Scenes of historic significance were flowing across the screen—the Roman army, Stalin, Madame Curie, Mao, Washington, Lee, and Lincoln; no images repeated. As I watched, a dialog box crystallized as it traveled from background to foreground.

Welcome to the World of Antiquity, Jeffery. You will find Antiquity is like no other game you've played.

Are you ready to begin?

I guess I was enamored with Antiquity's presentation and didn't consider the manner in which it had acquired my name. I pulled up my chair, took the mouse in hand, and selected "Yes." Another dialog box appeared.

Enter your Antiquity password

Enter my Antiquity password? There was no option to select one. *This is stupid*, I thought, but, as quickly as I made my declaration, an image of letters and symbols involuntarily formed in my mind. It was an odd feeling, like a projection in my brain. *How could it hurt?* I asked myself. So I keyed what I was seeing and pressed "Enter." I was in.

Another message appeared on the screen.

It is your turn. What event in history would you like to influence? We suggest you start with something small—the ripple effects of change can be profound.

Below this message, there was an entry box that looked like it would accept text. Instinctively, I typed four words. You would think I would have moved on, but the events of that day still burned.

Bring back my sister

My finger hovered over the "Enter" button as I stared at what I had typed. I didn't really believe the game could change history, but a creepy "I shouldn't do this" feeling came over me, and I backspaced over my words.

Okay, Antiquity, I thought, *my last English grade sucked; let's see what you can do.* I figured one English test, give or take, had to qualify as "small."

Change the result of my last English test to an A.

I reread what I'd typed, laughed, shook my head, and pressed "Enter."

The images on the screen started to change rapidly, until I couldn't distinguish one from the next. After a moment, the swirling slowed, and the image of a test—grade C— appeared on the screen, caught fire, and burned to glowing embers that died as ash. I rubbed my eyes, and, before they could readjust, the image was gone. A statement followed.

Your event is being administered. You will be notified when complete.

The game's screen rapidly collapsed into an icon on my desktop.

So, Antiquity likes to put on a show. What time is it? I thought as I looked toward the window. It felt like I had been sitting there an hour. I still needed to answer my last civics question. I tried my "Khan" search again, found a normal website, and patched together an answer. I solved the two remaining algebra questions and started to look for the software I wanted, but I struggled to find anything. I decided it would wait until tomorrow. I cleaned up, said my goodnights, started streaming a video on my tablet, and drifted away.

I awoke early, after an endless series of strange dreams, which was fortunate, because I'd forgotten to set the alarm. I jumped into the shower and stepped through the rest of my morning routine. I was ready to head out the door with a few minutes to spare, so I wiggled the mouse. I wanted to continue the software search. When I logged on, I saw Antiquity was back with another message.

Your event change is complete

"Sure it is . . . what a waste of time," I murmured.

I closed Antiquity and left for school.

Wednesday moved along like most Wednesdays. I was thankful it wasn't Monday, but Friday still seemed out of reach. The pop quiz in algebra caught me off guard, civics finished on an unimpressive note, and my old friend English was next. I rolled into class just before Miss Jenson closed the door. I planted myself in my usual spot, behind Susie Wentworth, who, in my opinion, was one of the hottest girls to walk the building—maybe a little sad, a little quiet, but hot, in a sophisticated sort of way. She was a straight-A's kind of girl and didn't make time for love, from what I'd heard. I fantasized about asking her out but always backed down when I had an opening. Asking girls out wasn't my strong suit. I had a girlfriend for a while in ninth grade, but when we broke up, I got into computers, and I mainly hung with my geek friends or played online.

I was coming out of my Susie haze when I realized Miss Jenson was walking the aisles, handing out papers. *Shit, another quiz.* This wasn't going to be pretty. I was behind on my homework and hadn't read the assigned chapter. Susie turned over her paper and made a small, almost-imperceptible gasp. *Great,* I thought, *if she thinks it's bad, I am totally screwed.* Aubrie was next to get a paper. She was another no-nonsense student who hadn't fallen from the top rankings since I'd first crossed her path in second grade. She turned toward Susie with a look of incredulity, holding her paper to show Susie a B-minus. Susie angled her paper so Aubrie could see—another B, though I couldn't see if it was the high or low variety. I was lost. Had I somehow missed a test? A quiz? And what happened to the A twins? I was trying to decipher this puzzle when Miss Jenson placed a paper on my desk face down. She looked at me and gave me an approving nod.

Miss Jenson meant her small overture to convey satisfaction, but satisfaction wasn't the feeling that filled my gut. "Confused" best described my current state. Something in my brain or heart—or both—nagged at me, and I had few clues as to why. I slowly turned my paper to its right side, and, there, in the upper left corner, stood an A-plus, circled for additional emphasis. As my eyes left the A-plus perched on the corner of my paper, I discovered something more. This paper, I should say a poorer variation, had been handed to me two days before.

As I read the words assembled on the page, they rang a familiar tone. They were my words, but not really mine. I was capable of stringing together the occasional well-crafted sentence, but this was good, really good, from top to bottom. How was it I could feel like the author and a plagiarist at the same time? How was it possible my newly minted paper was here in front of me and its inferior cousin, the original, was at home in my room? The final oddity was that every other student in the room should have had a second copy as well, but none of them had the recollection I did. As I lifted my eyes toward the front of the classroom, I noted both Susie and Aubrie were examining me and my composition with fascination, like I had kidnapped their A's. Aubrie interrupted the awkward moment with an equally awkward and insincere pronouncement: "Great job, Jeffery."

"Huh?" I grunted.

"Your paper, an A-plus," she said disbelievingly.

"I guess I got lucky," I said halfheartedly.

That brilliant bit of eloquence resulted in both my female classmates turning back toward our teacher, who was once again taking the helm. Not surprisingly, my focus was elsewhere for the balance of the class. I could hear Miss Jenson's voice, but it was babble in my brain. *No, no, no, it can't be . . . Antiquity.* Yet the paper on my desk belied my disbelief. There had to be a reasonable explanation that didn't involve a computer game.

"Jeffery. Jeffery."

I snapped back to consciousness with Miss Jenson's words echoing in my ears.

"Yes, Miss Jenson?"

"Jeffery, class is over."

"Sorry, I was distracted." I thanked Miss Jenson, packed up, and wandered into the hall.

I was surrounded by the usual end-of-day buzz as I shuffled down the corridor.

"Hey, geek," I heard Jason call from behind.

"Don't give me that 'geek' crap—you're the frick'n mayor of geeksville," was my sad comeback.

"That was lame," Jason said, knocking me off balance with a shove.

"I know—I've got to let you win sometimes," I retorted.

"In your dreams, dude," Jason laughed. "Seriously, you don't look good; you're whiter than usual."

"Something weird happened. I got an A-plus on an English paper, and I think this game I downloaded . . . Ah, forget it. I got to roll. I'll text you later," I said, moving toward the door.

"Really, man—you okay?" Jason asked sincerely.

"Yeah, I'm good. I'll catch up with you later." I turned, letting the door close behind me.

I wanted to get home and put my two papers side by side and have another sit-down with Antiquity. I couldn't explain what happened and had to find solid ground.

I usually nuked a Hot Pocket when I got home but decided to skip it. My stomach could wait. I opted to look for my first English paper. I dug through two days' accumulated clutter to find a blackened parchment. As I raised it for a better look, it disintegrated and rained ash on my feet. I sat in my chair and rubbed my hair as I struggled to think clearly. I rolled to my computer and moved the mouse, bringing my computer to life.

In the lower right-hand corner stood the Antiquity icon. I double-clicked the icon, launching the program.

A parade of spectacular images once again made their way across my screen. The same crazy password routine and the same dialog box soon followed, parking itself in the center of the screen.

What event in history would you like to influence?

This time, there was no suggestion to limit my influence to a small event. Apparently I had graduated. I looked around the screen and noticed a question mark begging my attention. I exercised the "Help" option, as I couldn't think of a more appropriate action, given the circumstances. A search field, along with a FAQ option, appeared. I chose FAQ.

The FAQ page began with five short sentences:

Few are given the chance to influence historical events. It is a privilege. It is possible to alter life's outcomes, however, you should consider your choices carefully. Antiquity reserves the right to disallow any change. The questions and answers that follow describe the bounds that Antiquity generally adheres to, but Antiquity will also behave unpredictably at times.

The questions followed:

Q: Can an event changed by a player be reversed?

A: An historical event can be influenced a maximum of two times, whether by the original player or another. However, changing historical events is exceedingly complicated, and an exact reversal is seldom possible. A player who chooses to reverse an historical event that has already been changed once will be penalized because of the difficulty involved in reversing an event. A minimum of one turn is required, but one turn may not be sufficient if a penalty is required. Antiquity reserves the right to inhibit or allow a second event change.

Q: Can the event of downloading Antiquity be reversed?

A: No, Antiquity has immunity, and no uninstall is possible, nor can an event change be used to inhibit Antiquity's function for any player.

Q: Are there others who are influencing historical events?

A: There are three others currently playing.

Q: Can players coordinate their efforts?

A: Yes.

Q: Can one player give their turns to another player?

A: This is allowed only when a player doesn't have enough turns to pay a penalty.

Q: Can I contact other players?

A: Yes. Antiquity also notifies all players, past and present, when a player has taken a turn. A description of the player's requested change is also given.

Q: Can Antiquity affect the lives of other players via event changes?

A: Yes, although not in a way that would invalidate the fact that Antiquity selected a player. For example, killing another player in a conventional manner, not in self-defense, would prevent the murdered player from continuing play. Therefore, penalties would be assessed against the aggressor. However, changes in history that happen around other players can affect their lives up to and including death. If a player dies, any remaining turns that player had are forfeited. Antiquity reserves the right to disallow any change.

Q: Must I participate?

A: A minimum of two turns must be played within a fortnight. You may, however, continue to play until your turns are consumed, a total of seven turns per player. Failing to fulfill your minimum obligation will result in Antiquity taking two turns for you. Antiquity advises against this course. Turns taken, turns remaining, and penalties imposed will be tracked and displayed for all players on Antiquity's home screen.

Q: Can I show others Antiquity and what it does?

A: Only current players or previous players can detect that changes in history have occurred. Showing anyone else will be meaningless because they won't remember the state of the world before. For this reason, a non-player will not believe the game had any effect. After all your turns are utilized, the game loses its ability to change past events, although current and previous players will continue to see notices.

Q: Is there a way to minimize unforeseen repercussions?

A: Antiquity's algorithm considers intent. A greed/altruistic quotient is applied which affects the waves created by any influenced event.

Q: Why me?
A: You were selected, Jeffery.

I minimized Antiquity and leaned back.

I was selected? Chill-bumps started on my scalp and moved halfway down my back before dissolving.

I reconsidered this afternoon's English class. Susie and Aubrie's low test scores—did I somehow take part of their grades? Again, I rubbed my head as I reasoned my next step. Judging from what I'd just read, I had to play again. There were three other players. What were they doing?

CHAPTER 2

LIGHT SHONE ON THE MOUNTAINS that stood like stony ramparts on an ancient castle. Yoko loved the mountainous terrain surrounding her home, but she no longer saw its beauty. The golden disk rising to her right was distorted and shimmered through the tears in her eyes. Although many had felt the wrenching pain of heartache, it was new to her. Although dating was expressly discouraged, she'd long considered Ren her boyfriend, and now he was pulling away. Her confidence was gone, and the "Why?" of it was beyond reach. She ceaselessly considered all she had done and all she had said, grasping to find some reason. A month ago, they'd talked of going to university together, and now her presence was scarcely acknowledged.

Yoko allowed herself to drift back in time, remembering when it was easy to be friends. She had known Ren since middle school. He moved to town when his father was transferred to a new position. She didn't think much of him when first they met. He was cocky and rudely outspoken.

Once, on a field trip, much to her dissatisfaction, they were seated together, and, in predictable fashion, Ren started his loud, obnoxious display. Yoko reacted by embarrassing him in front of the others. As a result, he stopped talking and said nothing for miles. Yoko elected to break the silence by apologizing for hurting his pride. To her surprise, Ren quietly started opening up. He talked of his older brother, the brother he idolized, who'd been killed in a climbing accident when Ren was just eight. She began to look at Ren differently afterwards, realizing his act was a means of forgetting, of hiding his pain.

In the days and months that followed came hallway smiles, locker talks, and mutual tables in the lunchroom. She talked to him of her feelings of not fitting in, a nagging insecurity she'd carried for as long as she could remember, though she was never able to identify any incident that would explain its genesis. He revealed that, despite his formidable achievements in school, he felt his success required twice the effort when compared to that of his classmates. Yoko was deeply compassionate and helped Ren look at life and loss differently. And Ren, for his part, helped Yoko gain confidence and helped her feel she did have a place.

As each year passed, they grew closer. Ren matured and softened, though he didn't completely lose his smart-ass ways, which Yoko found amusing. He always made her laugh. They never had a serious argument she could remember, and they were inseparable. When news of their relationship's demise spread, all were shocked. Yoko was asked repeatedly if it was true, and, each time, it forced her to acknowledge it.

Her friends were sympathetic, inviting Yoko to movies and similar outings, but there was no place that provided comfort—when alone, she wanted to be with friends; when with friends, she wanted to be alone. Her mother said she would feel better in time, and though her mother meant well, common-sense advice was of little consolation. Yoko wanted things to be as they were but could find no way back.

Presently she sat staring at a computer screen, about to play a game that claimed she could alter events. She didn't believe it possible, but she knew at least one other person was playing because of the message she'd received. She thought this fantasy might provide some relief. She slowly typed her heart's pressing desire:

Restore my relationship with Ren.

Yoko pressed "Enter."

She felt strange after electing this choice. Prior to their breakup, she'd learned from her friends that Ren was spending time with a new circle, a circle which included one of the prettiest girls in school. As she tried to make sense of what she was feeling, Antiquity provided its feedback, which broke her contemplation.

Your event is being administered. You will be notified when complete.

Yoko left her room and walked to the family room, where her mother and father were sharing their sofa, each reading books purchased on a recent trip to their favorite bookstore.

Tatiana stared at the laptop given to her by her uncle, Andrei, who had passed away two years prior. It was an older model, but to Tatiana, it was miraculous. The internet opened doors to a world she found astonishing, a world so unlike the desolate wintery Russian town in which she lived.

Life hadn't been easy for Tatiana, her sister, or her mother. Her father left them shortly after her ninth birthday. Calling him "father" was a misnomer, as he generally spent evenings drinking with friends. On the days he was home, he was impatient and, on more than one occasion, struck her or her sister under the pretext of teaching discipline. Looking back now, she understood his foul attitude was largely the result of the previous night's fondness for vodka. He never behaved as if he were part of the family, rather, he fancied himself an intellectual with no time to waste on wife or children. Her mother tried to make up for his lack of involvement through sheer effort, exhausting herself by carrying the burden of keeping house and rearing their two daughters.

Despite his poor fathering, Tatiana blamed herself for his departure, as did her sister. There was no sound logic that proposed either Tatiana or her sister Alena bore responsibility for his choice to walk away, but they accepted it nonetheless. They weren't alone; those left in the wake of abandonment always seem to pay the higher price. Tatiana's mistrust of the opposite sex was another byproduct of her father's behavior that would haunt her. For this reason, she never allowed herself to grow close to any male, no matter the boy's intentions. She would deliberately distance herself if she felt her protective wall at risk. Tatiana had twice tried seeing boys she found attractive but pulled away so abruptly that the shunned young men labeled her "crazy" and warned others who considered chancing a date. The talk circulating in school hurt her, but she didn't show pain, choosing to remain stoic in the face of whispers and jeers. In her heart, there was a growing fear she might never manage to rid herself of the ghosts of her father's influence. Each time those fears began to take hold, she would find a new distraction. This time, she'd found a game.

When Tatiana chose to download Antiquity, she never imagined it would result in the hospitalization of her older sister. Now there were dark circles under her eyes, certainly partly hereditary, but sleepless nights weren't helping. Her initial belief that the game would be fun and would contribute to her learning about her favorite subject had now been replaced with the understanding it was no game, at least not by any convention she appreciated.

Tatiana influenced an event the day she downloaded Antiquity, and what occurred had frightened her. Tatiana's choice arose from a stupid argument she'd had with her younger sister, Alena. Tatiana had given Alena an idea for a school paper, for which Alena received her mother's and her teacher's adulation, and Tatiana felt she deserved more credit for helping Alena find her motivation. Tatiana loved her sister deeply, but in a moment of anger, she chose to take back the idea she had given Alena when the game asked which event Tatiana wished to influence. Tatiana never thought the game's assertion possible and looked at her decision to select this event more like therapy—a chance to release her frustration.

She typed her request and pressed the "Enter" key. She felt a pettiness as she lay down and pulled up her quilts.

"I will feel better tomorrow," she said softly and closed her eyes.

Tatiana awoke the next day to find her computer screen displaying a message:

Your event change is complete.

She shrugged it off, as she had chores to do that Saturday and began the day's work.

Tatiana was cleaning her room when Alena walked in and asked for ideas for a history paper due the upcoming Tuesday. Tatiana froze as a feeling of déjà vu momentarily overwhelmed her. She recognized life was replaying itself, and she sat on the bed she was making.

"Are you alright?" Alena asked when she saw the odd expression on Tatiana's face.

"Yes," Tatiana responded as she gathered herself. "I'm sorry I can't think of any ideas," Tatiana said as she got up to finish making her bed.

"Not a problem," Alena said. "I'm going to the library to see if I can find a topic. Let me know if you think of anything."

Tatiana's selfish act gave her a hollow feeling, and she turned to follow, but she heard the front door swing shut and decided not to pursue it further. Tatiana rational- ized her action, thinking it would be good for Alena to develop her own idea. She went on with her work, but as the day wore on, she couldn't rid herself of the guilt. She decided she would share her idea when Alena came home, but Alena didn't return home that Saturday afternoon. Alena was run down when a vehicle rounded a corner too quickly. Although Alena's injuries were not life threatening, her broken leg required surgery to reposition and pin the bones.

Tatiana wanted to tell Alena and her mom what had happened, but she didn't think they would believe her. She was sick with shame. Now home from visiting her sister, she wondered what to do. Tatiana contemplated reversing what she had done, but Antiquity's assertion that an exact reversal was "seldom possible" troubled her. She supposed things could worsen. By the game's rules, she had to play at least twice within two weeks. She had read all the FAQs and wondered what the other players were doing and thinking, and if they had chosen selfishly.

Tatiana pondered her next move. As she considered her options, a thought occurred to her. One of her friends, a classmate, had dropped out of school to help at home because her mother had fallen ill. Tatiana often worried about her friend. Perhaps now Tatiana could do something to help. She didn't know if an unexpected problem would arise out of this attempt at good, but, regardless, this choice wouldn't be a selfish one.

Tatiana logged on and started Antiquity . . .

***

Player Mystic has influenced an event improving the health of a girl's mother.

The fourth participant was considering his first play when he read the notification. Though he scarcely believed the game was more than a toy, he scoffed at what he considered a waste of imagination. Should this game actually have the power to change outcomes, he would put it to use. Starting small was like throwing a feather to the breeze. He would throw a rock in a river. If he were able, he would seek revenge for those he considered wronged by America and its "stooges." He was mission-bound to seek retribution on behalf of the rest of the world. He intended to dole out justice, despite the fact that his knowledge of history lacked substance.

He'd recently read of an airliner saved from mid-air doom when a bomb was discovered in the cargo hold prior to the plane leaving the ground. Thanks to an extraordinary level of international cooperation and good local investigative work, the bomb's construction was traced back to a known terror cell, and multiple arrests were made.

The failure of the planned downing infuriated him, and though he felt his interaction with Antiquity would provide only a virtual reckoning, he would pretend with vigor.

He felt no remorse when he typed his request below Antiquity's invitation:

The bomb discovered on flight 5249 must go undetected and detonate as planned.

Methodically, he pressed "Enter."

Real or not, the lives on that airplane meant nothing to him. Although he wished his request would be granted, lashing out by means of a game gave him a sense of victory. He stretched out and had no difficulty falling into a deep sleep.

The sound of his mother's screams jarred him to consciousness. Still disoriented from being disturbed in so abrupt a fashion, he summoned the effort and got to his feet to talk to his mother.

"What, mother? What's wrong?" he asked harshly. His mother was so distraught it took repeated requests before she was able to express herself.

"Your cousin!" she sobbed.

"What about my cousin?" he pressed.

"He was traveling with his family," she said, weeping uncontrollably.

"What happened?" he said, holding her by her shoulders.

"He and his wife and their two young children . . . you remember them?"

"Yes—what happened?"

"The plane . . . the plane they were on," she said haltingly.

Her son's face changed, in both shade and demeanor.

"What happened, mother?"

"Their plane fell from the sky. A bomb. A terrorist has claimed it," his mother said as she folded in two, her knees meeting the floor with a dull thud.

He let her go and moved quickly to his computer. The screen illuminated.

Your event change is complete.

He shook his head in disbelief and launched his browser. His home page screamed with headlines of a downed plane, flight number 5249. He, too, bent and knelt, though he didn't feel pain as his knees touched his room's hard floor. *This cannot have happened,* he thought as he rocked slowly back and forth. *The enemy has tricked me. The Americans devised this elaborate scheme.* His rocking motion became erratic. "They have tricked me, mother."

His mother raised her face to him. "Who has tricked you, son?"

"Our enemies!"

"What do you mean, son?" she asked again. "Our cousins have surely perished. Did you not hear me, son?" she voiced with frustration. "What does this have to do with 'enemies'?"

"I shall have my vengeance!" he said, banging his fist on the desk.

"'Vengeance'—what do you mean, son?"

"You will understand."

To his way of thinking, he bore no responsibility. So deep was his hatred, so twisted his design of thinking, he began conceiving a plan before the blood of his cousin's family had had time to stain the earth.

CHAPTER 3

AS I CONSIDERED WHAT TO DO NEXT, my home page was busy exhibiting pane upon pane of the latest celebrity scandals, scores, and headlines. One particular headline, the loss of an airplane and everyone on-board, stood out prominently. Antiquity had displayed a message a few hours ago:

Player Sage has influenced an event involving an airliner, which will cost the lives of two hundred and sixty-three passengers and crew.

My God! Who could do this? One player helps a mother, and another is responsible for death! As questions churned in my mind, I considered something about Antiquity's FAQs.

Can I contact other players? The answer had been "Yes," with no elaboration. I wondered how it worked. I remembered seeing a search tool on Antiquity's help page. I launched Antiquity and once again accessed "Help."

I typed my question into the field.

A spinning disk appeared on the screen as Antiquity sought to answer my question. In a scant second, the answer was presented:

There is an email application which is accessed from Antiquity's home screen. It allows players to communicate. No player is obligated to communicate. The application preserves the player's anonymity and is capable of translating to any language if requested.

I closed the "Help" utility, returned to Antiquity's home screen, and found "Player Email" on a pull-down menu.

The email window opened, exposing a blank message. I clicked the "To" button, which displayed a small list. Player Solon, Player Mystic, Player Sage, Player Guru. Antiquity assigned names to each player. I had received event-change notifications from three players: Mystic, Sage, and Guru. Hell would freeze over before I emailed Sage. I decided to send a test email to Solon, aka me, to see if it worked. I typed a crap message and hit "Send." A few moments later, a notification popped up:

A player has sent you a message. Would you like to open it? Opening a message will not send confirmation to the sender.

I opened the email, and all looked as expected. I tried to drill deeper to see if one of my real email addresses was linked, but I found nothing. Given what psycho Sage had done, I was cautious. I figured Mystic might be safe, seeing as she had tried to help a family.

I opened an email and typed.

I'm an Antiquity player. What Sage did was some messed-up shit. I played only once, but it did what I asked. I don't know who else to talk to. Are you good with email?
Solon

I clicked "Send."

Leaning back in my chair, I folded my hands behind my head and turned my thoughts to the second turn I had to take. I watched images dance across the screen. I remembered hearing about a classmate whose home had been badly damaged by a fire about a week ago. A drunk at the wheel of a truck lost control and slammed into their home, causing a devastating fire. The Red Cross found the family temporary residence, and a group at school collected some essentials, but there had been nothing in the way of updates since.

I rolled to my keyboard and found the local paper's online site. I searched and found the detail I was looking for—the address, family name, and more. Antiquity was still up, its invitation planted squarely in the middle of my screen. I typed my event change:

Ensure the fire that burned the Ryan home located on Laramie Lane doesn't occur.

I pressed "Enter."

Your event is being administered. You will be notified when complete.

Resting my elbows on the desk, I closed my eyes and wondered if Mystic had read my email. I considered talking to my parents, but how do you tell someone who has no memory of what existed that a new reality had been created? *Yeah, I'll worry about that later.* My original English paper lay in ashes on my floor. Maybe altering the outcome of the house fire will leave a trail?

I stood, slid my feet into my slippers, and shuffled toward the kitchen.

———◆———

In calculus the next morning, Yoko sat at her desk and forced a smile as a friend walked by. Ren would normally sit in the desk immediately behind, but since making new friends, he had moved across the room. She briefly glanced to see if he was there but found his new seat empty. The teacher was writing a series of equations on the board when, from the corner of her eye, she saw Ren enter the room. To Yoko's surprise, he casually sat behind her, as if nothing had changed.

"What's wrong with you? Your face looks pale!" he said in a manner that didn't account for what had happened.

She turned to look at him, astonished that he'd asked the question.

"Where are Aiko and your new friends?"

"Aiko? New friends? Are you sick or something?"

"I thought you were enamored with . . . "

The teacher abruptly interrupted Yoko, instructing her to face forward.

"We'll begin," he said sharply.

Yoko felt calculus always dragged, but, on this particular morning, it more than dragged. Yoko's mind raced. She was so wrapped up with what had happened, it took a moment to remember Antiquity. She felt her face flush as she thought further. Class was finally coming to an end, and Yoko looked down at a blank page in her notebook. She closed it, stood, and saw Ren preparing to leave.

"Are you sure you're okay?" he asked as he gathered his books.

He walked with Yoko toward the door. Her heart was pounding. Yoko never imagined Ren would converse with her like he used to.

As life tends to, it conspired to place Aiko and her clique immediately outside the classroom. Yoko watched Ren with curiosity as Aiko looked on with coveting eyes. To her amazement, Ren paid no attention to Aiko and the others as they passed; still, there was something different about Ren that gave Yoko pause. She chose to push down her concern as she and Ren strolled down the hallway.

As the hours passed, Yoko continued to detect differences in Ren's behavior and attitude—a coldness and a distance prevailed. His words weren't so different, but the way he conveyed them was new. She didn't verbalize her thoughts, but the word "dead" formed in her mind. She suspected Antiquity had restored Ren's friendship, but only in part. Yoko was realizing the gift she'd been granted was no gift at all, and, as she left for home that afternoon, she knew what had to be done.

Though this had been a difficult, emotional day, when Yoko arrived home, she hung her coat and removed her shoes as she did every day. She walked down the hall toward her bedroom, barely acknowledging her mother's

"Hello." She opened her laptop and brought up Antiquity. From the home screen, she accessed "Help" and searched for: *influencing an event twice.*

Yoko read Antiquity's rule and the caveats. She hung her head, and, as she did, a single tear left her eye and fell to the keyboard. She closed the "Help" window and typed her event change:

Reverse my request to restore my relationship with Ren

Her finger lingered a moment over the "Enter" key before pressing it.

Antiquity's status message appeared on schedule:

Your event is being administered. You will be notified when complete.

The appetite which had recently deserted her showed an inkling of resurgence. Yoko left her room and followed the aroma of her mother's cooking to the kitchen. Yoko had done the right thing, and that alone provided a small measure of peace. She embraced her mother as she entered the kitchen. Her mother smiled and dipped a large spoon into the pot of soup simmering on the stove. Her mother carefully offered Yoko a taste of the golden broth.

CHAPTER 4

TATIANA WAS SURPRISED when she received Jeffery's—make that Solon's—email. The message was in English, and though Tatiana was proficient in English, she decided to exercise Antiquity's translation tool as a test. It changed the email to her mother language—Russian. As she finished reading, another Antiquity notification startled her.

Ensure the fire at the Ryan home located on Laramie Lane doesn't occur.

She nodded in approval after reading the notice.

Her last turn had resulted in what she'd hoped for. Her friend was back in school, although with a cast on her arm. She'd suffered the break while saving her mom from falling down a flight of steps. Tatiana questioned whether this was Antiquity's attempt to balance life's scales, but the net result was vastly better, in her opinion, and she chose not to devote further energy splitting hairs.

Tatiana turned her attention back to the email she was writing.

Solon,

Sage is evil. What else could it be? I'm reading rules and reading the notes when players take turns. Have you thought about working together . . . as a team? Do you have passwords in your head?

Mystic

Send.

———

True to his promise, Sage began devising a plan the very afternoon his mother had brought the news of his cousin's death.

He sat at his computer and searched site after site, poring over every news item he felt relevant. Sage was looking for the ideal event, something that would cause death and international calamity. Three times his mother entered his room, pleading with him to eat something; each time, he commanded she leave him to his work.

He stopped when an article about the International Space Station caught his eye. It described a foiled attack. As he continued reading, he learned that both American and Russian lives would have been lost. Investigators had found that a member of the team, responsible for the fuel systems, was working with a terrorist network. The plan was to alter the software used to control several key valves, thereby causing an immense explosion as the craft was docking. The scheme was discovered shortly before the June 3, 2018 flight.

He stood and paced the floor as he meditated.

He opened Antiquity and typed the following:

Make sure those trying to destroy the Space Station during the June 3, 2018, mission are successful.

He reread the request and pressed the "Enter" key.

Your event is being administered. You will be notified when complete.

He was pleased when he received Antiquity's notice.

His appetite suddenly returned.

Electing to go to the market, he was gone several hours. Sage returned with bags full of fresh fruit, vegetables, and a fine cut of lamb. His mother thanked him and smiled as she placed the produce in baskets she kept in the kitchen and the outer room. As she went about her tasks, she hoped to see some semblance of a peaceful demeanor in him. Her son's vengeful sentiments from earlier profoundly concerned her.

He selected a pear to his liking from his mother's basket and strode with purpose toward his room, rubbing the pear's skin on his pant leg as he walked. Sage expected to see that Antiquity had completed its work. He was surprised to see the same message on the screen:

Your event is being administered. You will be notified when complete.

Initially concerned, he considered the immense complexity of changing history, even the smallest event, and relaxed, electing to close his laptop.

"I'm going to bed," he called from his room.

"Sleep well, son," his mother said as she walked to his doorway, hoping to see a brightness in his eyes, but he wouldn't meet her gaze.

Another restless sleep, and I was feeling it. I moved toward my computer but then backed away—I wasn't ready for the crazy shit going on out there. There was a noise down the hall, and I journeyed toward the kitchen. As I neared the kitchen, I recognized the sound of mom's old-school radio. I hadn't heard it in a long time. She was listening to the news. Normally it was TV news. Something was different. I sat down at the table across from her. She was drinking coffee, and the aroma filled the room.

"I want some coffee this morning," I said, expecting her to say that I hated coffee, but she didn't respond.

I looked at her and could see she was distracted.

"What's wrong, mom?"

"What did you say, Jeffery? I'm sorry, sweetheart. My mind was elsewhere."

"You seem sad."

"I don't mean to be down, honey. The news is so disheartening. The kids are being drafted, and sometimes it seems like we'll never get things straightened out," she said faintly.

I looked at her like she had lost it.

"Are you really okay?" I asked, filling my mug with more cream than coffee.

"Yes, honey. I'm distracted. Did you need anything?"

"No, I'm good," I said as I gave her a hug.

The kids are being drafted? I found the last of the chocolate-chunk cookies and picked up my mug. I parked at my desk and brought up Antiquity. There was a notification.

That son of a bitch—Sage.

My eyes narrowed as I reread Antiquity's two notices:

Player Guru has influenced an event which will release her boyfriend from love's obligation.

Player Sage has influenced an event involving the destruction of The International Space Station.

Whoever Sage is, something is way wrong in his head, I thought. *It's got to be a dude; I don't think chicks peddle that brand of crazy.*

But how did this lead to *the draft?*

I Googled "space station" and started reading. The station was no more. The explosion that rocked the man-made island caused severe damage at the point of the blast but also caused a shift in its orbit. The scientists below were unable to stabilize the craft, and it collided with a satellite—not just any satellite, but Russian-military-design newly launched. Both craft entered the atmosphere spiraling to their premature ends.

Lives were lost, and the Russians blamed America, describing it as a scheme to reduce Russia's military capability. Never mind that an American had been lost as well; in Russia, the widely circulated propaganda compared his loss to that of a lamb slaughtered to achieve a larger, more-sinister purpose. This calamity was followed by the downing of an American military transport miles from Russian airspace. Perhaps escalation could have been avoided had the two countries not already been at each other's throats over Syria, hacking, and so on. Too late for cooler heads, the Russian military mobilized their forces on Europe's doorstep, and NATO was obliged to stand united. The United States, otherwise occupied in other theaters, had instituted a draft to raise the necessary personnel.

I thought about the articles describing the series of events leading to the world's precarious position. How was it possible for mom, for anyone, not to remember another past? It was creepy.

I wanted to know how my request to save my classmate's home now read in the media. I called up the same website I used to find the Ryans' home. I found the local paper's website, but the story had changed. The drunk driver who had collided with their home and caused the fire was still at fault, but his car hit the Ryans' car in the driveway, missing their home. No fire had resulted, and the driver was arrested. While I digested this, another thought occurred to me. *What happens to all the printed material? Certainly Antiquity hasn't burned every newspaper in town, as had been the fate of my English paper.*

I stood and made a direct path for the cabinet that housed a stack of newspapers more than a month high. Digging through the ponderous assortment, I found what I was looking for. I unfolded the newspaper that should contain a report of the fire and not the driveway collision. I turned page upon page until I located the article. The print was distorted, and although smudges made it difficult to read, the article I read reflected the change I'd requested of Antiquity.

I walked back to my room, frequently stopping along the way, while I contemplated how Antiquity could alter all forms of media and memory—all memory with the exception of mine and the other players'.

My history teacher once taught us how wars start. How one event led to others—he called it "the domino effect." Now the dominoes were falling in my time. I should have done something to reverse Sage's first act of butchery and I wasn't about to let this stand. I was pissed. I restarted Antiquity. When it finished its startup routine, it alerted me that I had an unread email. It was from Mystic.

CHaPTeR 5

YOKO WOULD FACE HARD DAYS and nights still, but she knew her decision was the right one, and now she had even greater motivation. She saw what Sage had done and how it had changed the world. Yoko had grown up in a pacifistic Japan, yet even its troops were readying for war. She had received an email from the player called Mystic. She reread Mystic's email, which stood open on her screen.

Guru,

Everything is terrible here. No one except for me remembers the way it was before Sage. I wrote Solon and told him we need to work together. I don't know if we can make things right again, but we need to try. I think we need to save our turns to stop him.

Mystic

Yoko considered what Mystic was proposing. Sage had five turns remaining, and Antiquity wasn't black-and-white about how penalties would be applied. She blamed herself for using her turns carelessly, but she had no intention of wasting them now. The counter on her screen indicated she had used two turns and been penalized one. That meant that she had four left. Solon and Mystic had used two, leaving them five each.

Yoko opened a blank email and addressed it to Mystic and Solon. In the email, she agreed that they needed to form an alliance. She also made it clear that one of them had to reverse what Sage had started.

CHaPTeR 6

TATIANA READ GURU'S EMAIL and reviewed Antiquity's rule about reversing events. Another email arrived from Solon. Tatiana opened it and was surprised to see Solon was a boy named Jeffery.

Mystic and Guru,

I don't know how this is going to turn out, but I'm making a move. I'll use a turn to undo the nightmare Sage caused. When Sage figures out we're working together . . . I'm saying we need to be careful. I don't see that asshole stopping.

Something else: my name is Jeffery, and my picture is below. I looked up "solon," and I'm no statesman or advisor. I'm a kid in high school.

You'll see my change on your screens. And I don't understand how, but passwords appear in my head, too, as if they're being projected on a screen behind my eyes.

Jeffery

Tatiana thought Jeffery's decision to reveal who he was somewhat foolish, but it also interested her. She looked at his picture. Jeffery's hair was light brown, and several strands of his bangs were long enough to reach his right eye. His features were defined; his deep-set green eyes were captivating and serious looking, yet his smile was relaxed. She wondered if she could trust him.

Several hours later, Antiquity's notification flashed up on her screen:

Player Solon has reversed the event player Sage initiated concerning the Space Station.

CHAPTER 7

SAGE WAS PLEASED WITH HIS EFFORTS. To see the West ready to raise swords with Russia was more than he thought possible just a few hours ago. Although he didn't disdain Russia like he did America and its allies, he saw Russian involvement as a temporary measure—a stepping stone. He foresaw a world governed through strict religious adherence, a world where women were subservient to men, a world whose brutal disciplinary code for those who violated the law would right all that had gone wrong with the secular approach Western societies had adopted.

Sage had eluded the recent conscription in his own country because he was blind in one eye from an injury suffered as a boy. To those who asked, he claimed he pleaded with those in charge to allow him to join the military but was barred from doing so.

Sage planned on resting well that evening, but a disturbing dream awakened him shortly after midnight. His heart was pounding, and he was wet from sweating. In his nightmare, his vision of a new world had come to fruition, but the governed masses weren't content. Instead, the populace was lethargic. Everyone he encountered in the dream was blind. He happened upon his mother, and her warm face was now pale and gaunt. Her eyes were bloody, as if they'd been gouged by an animal. He didn't understand what the dream was meant to convey, but it left him with a deep sense of unease.

He stood and shuffled to the kitchen in the shadowy light of early morning to refill his flask with water. He drew a long drink, still affected by his dream—he struggled to shake off how real it seemed. As he returned to his bedroom, he opened his laptop to see if there was any news of war. He assumed that, by now, shots could have been fired.

Antiquity's screen appeared.

Player Solon has reversed the event player Sage initiated concerning the International Space Station.

Sage squinted as he focused his one good eye on the notice now occupying his screen. As its meaning penetrated, his hand let loose the flask he held. Water spread across the floor and pooled around his bare feet.

He quickly called up his preferred news sites and found nothing about an impending confrontation. He checked Al-Jazeera, CNN, Reuter's, and the BBC—nothing. He raised his hands to his head and pulled at his hair in intense frustration. At that moment, he swore he would find Solon and kill him.

The change in world order he desired was not to occur, at least not yet.

Sage opened an email message:

Solon,
You will regret this. You should have let my measures unfold without interference.
Sage

Sage remembered what he considered a pathetic use of a turn. Solon had saved a family from losing their home to fire. Sage kept track of all his co-players' turns, both the nature and the number of them. He opened the leather sleeve used to store his notes and read down the list. He read the note he was looking for: the Ryan home on Laramie Lane. Tomorrow he would call a man he knew, a man who specialized in finding people.

CHAPTER 8

I ROSE THE NEXT MORNING and looked out my window. It looked like any other morning, a normal day's beginning. As I rubbed my eyes, it occurred to me that the word "normal" no longer fit. I walked to the kitchen and found mom sitting at the table, sipping her coffee. The radio was off, and her face was bright, nothing like the careworn face of yesterday.

"No war worries this morning?"

"War worries?" she said, giving me a "Have you lost it?" look. "Do you want me to make you some breakfast?"

"No, I've got it," I said, as I slid out of the kitchen with a bowl of cereal. I ate my way back to my room, losing a few Cheerios along the way.

An email had arrived since I had last checked my inbox. I opened the message Sage had sent and read the two sentences he'd composed. I could feel his intensity. I pictured Sage honing a knife blade on a grinding wheel, like the Grim Reaper. I forwarded the message to Mystic and Guru. This hatin' dip-shit might come after them, too. From this point forward, we had to watch out for each other.

I Googled "Space "Station," and all was as it had been as far as I could tell. For a moment, I sat thinking about how our turns could be used if we didn't have to worry about fending off Sage. I broke away from thinking about what-ifs. It was good there were teachers' conferences today. I needed a day to chill. I wrote a second email.

Mystic and Guru,

Things here are better. No war, except between Sage and me. I don't think he wants to be friends. How are you? Have things settled down for you?

Do you see Antiquity's "scorekeeper"? I have three turns left, and Sage has five. Antiquity nailed me an extra point to clean up Sage's mess.

Jeffery

I hit "Send," and just as I had done for days now, I rested back in my chair and considered all that had happened. Rather than asking *how* Antiquity was able to change history, as I had been, my mind was now asking *why*.

CHAPTER 9

YOKO RECEIVED JEFFERY'S EMAIL and composed a reply.

Jeffery and Mystic,

My country is better, but I have really bad news. My mom came home from the doctor, and she has cancer.

She didn't tell me what the doctor said—about how bad it might be—but I'm scared.

What do I do? I have a chance to change this, but if I use my turns to help mom, we may not be able to stop Sage. I have only four turns left.

Yoko

Yoko pressed "Send" and went to find her mom.

CHAPTER 10

TATIANA READ HER EMAILS—first, the two Jeffery had sent. Then, one from a girl named "Yoko." She considered the choice facing Yoko. Tatiana wondered what she would do if faced with the same situation: Use a turn to save your mom, who gave you life and saw you through hell and high water, or conserve turns, in case they were needed to stop a psychopath.

Tatiana pulled her laptop toward her and began to type.

Jeffery, Yoko,

My name is Tatiana. I live in a small Russian town. My country is as it was before Sage.

Did you go back to the site where you found Antiquity? I tried, but the site was gone.

Yoko, help your mom. There is no choice. We will stop Sage.

I know someone is following me.

Tatiana

She got up and stood beside her window, carefully moving the drapery just enough to look at the street. No one was there, but she trusted her instincts. Someone was observing her, and she was going to find out who and why.

CHAPTER 11

SAGE WAS HAGGLING WITH A MAN, a man his mother had never met. The tone of their voices was serious and at times elevated. After several minutes, it quieted, with the pair reaching agreement on price.

Sage put all he knew on the table. "I feel this 'Solon' is a boy and probably in his teens. Second, I suspect he lives near a family with the last name of 'Ryan.' Third, the Ryan home is on a road named 'Laramie Lane.' Fourth, there may be a record of an accident occurring at the Ryan home. Finally, the boy mentioned a recent score of "A," received in an English class. I surmise such a result may be unusual for him—at least in English. Can you access school records?" Sage asked, intently.

The man nodded. "Yes, though the methods we use may not be entirely legal. The remainder of the data mentioned will be readily available. And you need this information when?"

"Quickly, but be thorough; cut no corners. I need precise information."

"Give me two weeks' time," the man said as he placed his hand on Sage's shoulder. "I will be in touch."

Sage escorted his guest to the door, opened it, and moved to the side to allow the man to step across the threshold. After closing the door, Sage turned to find his mother, looking at him with apprehension.

"Who is he?"

"A business acquaintance."

"What kind of business is he in, son?"

"He is helping me find an old friend; don't worry," Sage murmured as he poured a cup of tea. "There is nothing to lose sleep over."

His mother didn't believe him but didn't press further. She felt she no longer knew her son. As for losing sleep, she hadn't slept well for some time.

CHAPTER 12

AFTER READING TATIANA AND YOKO'S EMAILS, I opened another.

Tatiana and Yoko,

Yoko, I agree with Tatiana—help your mom. If you can use this game to do some good, you need to.

I've been thinking more about Sage. Anyone who can kill so indiscriminately wouldn't be bothered if there was one less Jeffery. He might come after me or one of you. So I have a question: Should we email each other every day? Just a word or two saying things are cool.

One other thing:

I live outside of Lexington, Virginia, USA. My full name is Jeffery McGregor. If I suddenly stop emailing, please let someone know.

Jeffery

I hit "Send." Thirty seconds later, my mom called for me. "What's up?" I yelled as I left my room to find her.

CHAPTER 13

SAGE OPENED THE DOOR to the man he'd hired to locate Solon.

"You will be pleased with the results of our efforts, my friend," the man said as he stepped into the room. "I have much to share with you."

"Come with me." Sage pointed, escorting the man past his mother. "We will talk in my room." Sage closed the door to his room and cleared a chair to make a seat for his visitor.

The man sat and opened a weathered leather case, removed a stack of documents, and arranged the pages at their feet.

"Let me explain," the man said as he admired the investigative work lying in front of them. "I feel we have located the person you are seeking—we are quite certain. I will show you," he said as he ordered the documents.

"We searched roads named "Laramie Lane," cross-checked against 'Ryan,' and found only one such combination in Virginia, USA. We then examined news sites and found a recently published article in *The News-Gazette*. The article describes a drunken driver who collided with a vehicle in the driveway of the Ryan home. We looked at the public schools which serve the Ryan neighborhood and found one. We were easily able to access school records. They need to employ me to secure their data. It took little effort—I almost feel guilty," the man expressed with an egotistical laugh.

"The Ryan boy attended a school in which another boy recently received an "A" in English. This was a departure from his typical "B" test scores. This second boy's family name is McGregor. We accessed credit-card records and found a recent video-card purchase. We were also able to track recent internet traffic. For reasons we cannot explain, your boy, Jeffery McGregor, recently downloaded something from a website that no longer exists. 'Khan' was the name we uncovered, but we couldn't ascertain the download, which is very unusual. Finally, we were able to access content from his Facebook page."

The man handed Sage a printout of a Facebook entry Jeffery had made.

"You see," the man grinned, "this is a picture of the boy you are pursuing. We have also provided his address and phone numbers."

"Excellent work. This has exceeded my expectations. Now that you have located him, I have another request."

"How can I help?"

"I understand there will be an additional fee," Sage said as he looked intently at the man.

"Yes, of course."

"I want to send this Jeffery another video card, of a very special design. Let me explain."

CHAPTER 14

YOKO CURLED UP ON THE SOFA beside her mother. She had learned more about the cancer assaulting her mother's body. It was in her liver. Normally, Yoko's mom was optimistic and energetic, but she hadn't managed a smile since her diagnosis. Each of the last two afternoons, after returning from school, Yoko had taken it upon herself to cook and clean, so that her mom could rest. The doctors were to start treating her tomorrow, but the prognosis wasn't favorable.

Yoko stood, covered her mother with a blanket, and shuffled down the hall to her room—she wanted to see what Antiquity's scoreboard said. She launched Antiquity, entered the password, and waited until the home screen appeared.

	Turns Taken	Penalties	Turns Remaining
Solon	3	1	3
Mystic	2	0	5
Guru	2	1	4
Sage	2	0	5

Yoko thought through the possibilities: *First, I help mom. Then Sage creates havoc with four of his five remaining turns. I and my new friends reverse every hateful thing Sage does. After that, even if Antiquity exacts only the minimal penalty, Sage would have one turn left, and Tatiana and Jeffery would each have one.*

Yoko put her elbows on her desk and sighed. *The rules say that a player can give away turns to cover penalties, but Tatiana and Jeffery will have only one turn to offer each other. Will that be enough?*

She remembered her commitment to stay in touch with the others. Yoko opened an email and began to write.

Tatiana and Jeffery,

Things have been quiet, but it feels like the calm before another storm.

My mom has liver cancer, and it doesn't look good. She is so depressed.

I have looked at the turns that each player has left. I'm afraid Sage will do something horrible, and we won't be able to stop him if I use a turn to help mom.

I want you to know I live in Nagano City, Japan. My full name Is Yoko Yamagata.

Yoko

Yoko pressed "Send" and went back to help her mother.

CHAPTER 15

TATIANA OPENED YOKO'S EMAIL. In her reply, she included Jeffery, as she had committed to write each day.

Yoko,
If you don't use a turn to help your mom, then I will!
The quiet worries me, too.
I'm joining you and Jeffery. I want you to know me.
I live in an area of Russia called Tura, and my name is
Tatiana Smirnov.
Tatiana

Send.
Tatiana was preparing to go to the hospital. Her sister was to be released, and she wanted to be there. Her family didn't own a car, but one of the neighbors offered to drive and would be arriving shortly. She finished putting her hair up and took her warm woolen coat from her closet. It wasn't stylish, but it was perfect for the long, cold winters.

Tatiana's mother opened their door to greet their kindly neighbor, whose name was Alexei. She invited him in for tea. Tatiana poured from the same pot her grandmother had when she was young and offered Alexei some sugar, which he declined, saying he liked his tea black.

Everyone was in high spirits knowing that Alena was coming home, and they all laughed and gossiped about the corrupt local officials, which was a favorite pastime. Tatiana did her best to embrace the mood, but the burden of the game and the nagging feeling she was being pursued by someone, or something, continued to weigh. After a few cups of hot tea, they pulled on their coats and left for the hospital.

When they arrived, Tatiana's mother proceeded to the counter where releases were processed. Tatiana took the stairs to the second floor and walked to the end of the cor-ridor, where she found the door to her sister's room open. Alena's things were packed, and Alena smiled broadly when she saw Tatiana. "How are you, Alena?" Tatiana asked as she wrapped arms around her sister.

"I'm so happy to be coming home," Alena declared, her eyes giving her emotions away.

"I'm so happy. I missed you. Mom is making your favorite for dinner."

"It felt like this day wouldn't come . . . I couldn't sleep last night," Alena smiled.

"We will be home soon. May I use your bathroom?" Tatiana asked, laughing as she added, "Too much tea." In the restroom, she heard a man's voice and assumed it was the doctor.

"Was that the doctor I heard?"

"No, another man. He said he knows you."

"What did he look like? Where did he go?" Tatiana asked hurriedly.

"He came and went so quickly. I really didn't pay attention. He stepped in, said he knew you, that you were friends, and then dropped off his card and walked out," Alena answered. "He put his card on the table. Is something wrong?"

"I'm sorry, Alena. I'm on edge today," Tatiana replied as she walked to the table and picked up the card. On its face was the name of a restaurant. She turned it over.

I know what's going on. I have seen the changes, your friend's mother, the space station. It is important that I speak to you. I need to leave the country for a few days, but I will find you when I return.

She stared at the card, her thoughts racing.

Her mother startled her as she entered the room. "Are you ready to come home, Alena?" her mother asked, smiling warmly.

"Yes, mom, I am," Alena said as she returned the smile.

"Tatiana, please pick up Alena's bag. I will push the chair," their mother said, walking to the back of Alena's wheelchair.

Tatiana mindlessly followed her mother's instruction. As they left the room, Tatiana looked in both directions . . . nothing but patients, nurses, and the echoes of their voices.

CHAPTER 16

SITTING IN THE SCHOOL CAFETERIA, thinking about the Antiquity crazy, I pictured Sage lying hidden, like a snake in tall reeds. Someone like Sage doesn't stop and walk away.

At Tatiana's urging, Yoko used a turn to help her mom. The cancer was gone, but her mom ended up with a case of pneumonia. Yoko said her mom was hurting, but compared to liver cancer, they could manage.

And then there was the card left for Tatiana by her unknown visitor—it freaked us out. She had been right all along—someone *was* watching, and whoever it was knew Antiquity. We all made guesses about who it might be: could it be another player whom Antiquity was keeping secret? At the worst, it could be Sage himself or a similarly deranged player.

As I walked home after school and turned the last corner, I could see our house in the distance. It sat on a cul-de-sac. My sister taught me to ride my bike on that round of pavement. I wondered if she was looking down from above.

Lately, I'd been missing her more. I used to talk to her when I was in trouble, and I could use her advice now.

Nearing our property, I looked on with fresh eyes. Ours was a mix of stone and lap siding with a chimney on the left side. The masonry on the chimney twisted artistically toward its highest point. There were two maples in the front yard that hadn't lost their brilliant orange foliage. The lawn was a blanket of green, and flower boxes hung beneath each of the front windows. The front door was mahogany, but its rich red color was partially obscured. I adjusted my focus to see a package—the familiar FedEx logo on its side. *My folks must have ordered something.* I could see from the label that the package had been shipped from the company that sent my video card. I figured it was a duplicate shipment.

I picked up the package and carried it inside. I dumped my bag on my bed and opened the box. A notice on company letterhead lay on top of another bubble-wrapped video card. The letter said that they had discovered a flaw in one of the chips on the first card and sent this updated version. *That's cool,* I thought . . . *how many companies would do that?* I finished my snack and installed the new card. I turned on my computer.

There was an odd smell and then a flash lit up my computer case. Then a ball of fire filled the room and knocked me off my chair. There was the sound of sirens and my ears ringing. I felt like I was on fire. I wanted to move, but my arms and legs wouldn't obey. I called out . . .

Tatiana,

Have you heard from Jeffery? I sent my email, and I got yours, but nothing from him.

Yoko

Yoko went about her day, assuming Jeffery was busy and would email shortly. Tatiana and Yoko agreed to give him hell for causing this angst. After writing several times more and receiving no response, Tatiana found Jeffery's Facebook page and looked for a recent posting, with no luck. Jeffery's parents were on Facebook as well, but there was nothing relating to a problem with Jeffery. Tatiana and Yoko continued to exchange information as each tried to track him down.

Jeffery had said he lived outside of Lexington, Virginia, so they began to search for more conventional information—phone numbers, an address, anything that could give them a lead. Tatiana found an address, but there was no public phone number listed. Yoko found a local news site for the Lexington area, but, so far, nothing had been reported concerning Jeffery. Reasoning they would think clearer with a few hours' rest, they set aside their keyboards and tried to sleep.

Yoko woke the following morning, pulled back the blankets, and sat on the edge of her bed. The house was cool, and she shivered as she slid her feet into her favorite pair of slippers, got up, and shuffled to her desk. As she entered her password, she was certain she would see an email from Jeffery. Unfortunately, Antiquity brought no news—good or bad.

Her stomach was empty, and it grumbled. She clicked the link she had saved to the local online newspaper—and found an article. "Oh, my God!"

Though her mother was still in bed, she heard Yoko and called out, asking what had happened.

"A friend of mine may have been hurt."

"Who?"

"He's a friend I met online," Yoko hedged, "You wouldn't know him."

"What happened to him?"

"I'm not sure," Yoko hesitating as she read.

The article provided scant detail. It described an explosion at Jeffery's address but said little else. The last line read: "An investigation was ongoing." There was no mention of injuries or casualties.

Yoko opened another email, gave Tatiana a brief update, and sent the newspaper's link.

———◆———

Tatiana sat up and rubbed the sleep from her eyes. Her brain was beginning to gather itself, and Jeffery's whereabouts was the first cohesive thought that formed. She could hear her mother rustling in the living room, and it sounded like she was stoking the fire. In the cold months, her mother liked to keep a fire alive, not only for heat, but because her mom said a fire welcomed all who entered.

Tatiana got to her feet, woolen socks still on, and slowly walked to the kitchen for hot tea and toast. She wished her mom a good morning but didn't stay to chat. Back in her room, she looked to see if there was any word from Yoko or Jeffery. She followed the link to the newspaper. Since Yoko had last read the article, there had been two updates of importance. One, the FBI was now investigating the incident, and, two, a person had been injured, but the article elaborated no further. Tatiana's heart sunk as she pictured Jeffery hurt and lying in a hospital.

Her mind was racing with questions. Was he the injured person? How could they find him? How did this happen? Was it Sage? They couldn't use a turn to help him without knowing something more. Maybe he was okay and couldn't email because of what had happened at his house. Maybe this wasn't because of Antiquity. Too many questions, too many maybes—she had to learn more.

She opened another email and wrote Yoko.

<hr>

Sage also found the Lexington local paper online and studied it closely. As he read the breaking news, a sense of satisfaction for a job well done rose within. An explosion had occurred, and a person had been injured. It had to be him. Part of the home had been destroyed. Authorities were not yet certain what had caused the blast. An investigation was ongoing. Every aspect of his plan had been achieved. *Jeffery should not have interfered. He brought this on himself,* Sage rationalized.

He felt fresh motivation and began anew to find an event he could turn to his favor.

CHAPTER 17

AFTER READING TATIANA'S EMAIL and the Lexington news, Yoko began searching for hospitals in the Lexington area.

Yoko let Tatiana know she was going to contact hospitals and ask for any information they were willing, or allowed, to provide. Tatiana responded quickly and suggested they say they want to have a gift or flowers delivered. Tatiana hoped someone would be sympathetic and indicate Jeffery was a patient. Though Tatiana hated the thought, she suggested they find hospitals with burn units. They compiled the short list, and each took half.

Eventually, their parents would ask why they'd called the United States, but that wasn't today's worry. Yoko completed her calls first and emailed Tatiana—no success. Tatiana's first call yielded nothing. She dialed the last number and prayed as the call's delayed connection went through. The woman who answered the call had an understanding voice, and Tatiana's quaver and heartfelt words softened the nurse's voice even more so. Tatiana asked her question and emphasized how important it was. The nurse told Tatiana she could send the flowers and said further she would personally see to it that Jeffery received them. She thanked the woman, and, wanting to know more, reluctantly said, "Goodbye." The emotion Tatiana felt surprised her, and it took a moment to shake it off. She shared what she'd discovered with Yoko. Several emails later, they agreed that using a turn to reverse what had occurred was their only recourse.

Yoko watched her screen. If something went wrong, Yoko planned to use one of her remaining turns. Tatiana and Yoko knew Jeffery would do the same if their positions were reversed. In short order, a notification appeared.

Player Mystic has influenced an event to set back the explosion which injured Player Solon.

I was walking home from school and could see a package on the front stoop. This scene was oddly familiar. I picked up the package and carried it inside. I opened the box and found a video card and a letter from the company explaining the reason for the shipment. I set down the card and letter, unloaded my gear, and grabbed a snack. I circled back, picked up the box, and made way for my room. In less than a minute, I loosened the thumb screw securing the tower's metal housing and set it aside. I pulled the old board, installed the new one, and buttoned things up. I plugged the cord into an outlet and reached for the power button, my finger stopping just short.

The sense of extraordinary familiarity grew in intensity. Every movement made, every angle viewed was a memory—it was either that or I was now able to see the future. THE BOARD IS RIGGED. I suddenly felt like a piece in a board game moved back eight places.

I remembered a flash and sirens. I remembered searing pain, the sort that can kill in and of itself. I pulled the cord from the wall and walked out my back door to breathe. As I paced, my mind cleared, and two plus two equaled four again. It was Antiquity, and my overseas friends had brought me back from death's door.

I considered talking to the police or the FBI or the CIA or some such ilk, but what could I tell them? *Some crazy asshole from I don't know where is trying to kill me because I'm messing up his plans to tear the world apart? And by the way, it's all happening because of a game that can change history.* That conversation would have to wait.

How do you throw something like this away? The town's reservoir? The garbage where some unsuspecting sanitation guy might get blown to hell? I removed the tainted board and repacked it. I stood over a package that had almost ended my life. There was an old pump house that sat just off our property that dad said the town bypassed years ago. When we were kids, we used to pry the door open just wide enough to get a look inside. We imagined zombies lived there; it was the perfect place to stow a bomb. I grabbed dad's pry-bar from the garage. I worked at it for a couple of minutes and managed to open the decrepit door just wide enough. I pushed the cardboard container though the spider webs and into the center of the small brick building. Another few minutes and two bruised shoulders later, the door was closed.

I walked back to the house and sat at my desk. I looked from left to right, taking an inventory of my stuff, appreciating my room. I had taken so much for granted, and now I knew how easily it could disappear. I took another bite of my PB&J, gulped down some milk, and pulled the keyboard closer. An email greeted me as soon as Antiquity finished its startup, followed by one sweet notification:

Player Mystic has influenced an event to set back the explosion which injured Player Solon.

Thank God for those girls—they saved my ass!

I read all their emails—they had copied me through the whole chain—smart, really smart. I wouldn't want them on the other side; that was for damn sure.

I clicked "Reply" on the last email in the string and typed.

Tatiana and Yoko,

How do you thank someone for saving your life? I would be dead now if it weren't for you. So I say "Thank you"—the biggest thank-you I've ever said.

That was crazy intense. One minute I'm fine, then I'm burnt toast, then I'm walking through some jacked-up Antiquity déjà vu.

You don't want to sign up for that thrill ride.

Be careful. Somehow Sage found me. Sage knew I bought a video card for my computer and had another one sent. All the paperwork looked official. I thought it was the real thing. When I turned the power back on, I guess it exploded. That's where everything gets hazy.

Please let me know how you're doing. Yoko, I know the name of your boyfriend was used when you played, and Sage knows you used a turn to help your mom. He might use this to find you.

Here's Antiquity's count.

	Turns Taken	Penalties	Turns Remaining
Solon	3	1	3
Mystic	3	1	3
Guru	3	1	3
Sage	2	0	5

If we can keep from getting assassinated, we might make it. I wonder if there's another way to look at this?
Jeffery

I hit the "Send" button when I heard mom unlocking the door. I met her as she stepped over the threshold and hugged her before she had a chance to set down her things.

"Well, that's a nice way to be welcomed home," she said with a smile. "What brought that on?" she asked.

"I don't let you know how much I love you."

"Teenagers," she laughed.

CHAPTER 18

TATIANA READ JEFFERY'S EMAIL and smiled. He was back. Tatiana took a deep breath and let out a sigh.

She lingered in the warmth of the moment until Antiquity alerted her that an email message had arrived. She opened the email. It was from Sage.

Mystic, Yoko,

You saw what happened to Jeffery. I strongly suggest you avoid interfering in the future. I have shown patience, but my patience has limits. I am certain you understand.

Sage

"Great. Now the devil himself is after me," she muttered, shaking her head.

Tatiana's religious beliefs were a reflection of her mother's, who'd always encouraged her and her sister to ask God for guidance. What was to come was uncertain, and she whispered a prayer, as her mom had taught, but she didn't know if it would be enough.

She decided to go for a walk to clear her head. What did Jeffery mean about "another way"? Had she exposed herself in some way that would allow Sage to find her? Could he find Yoko? Where was her mystery "friend"?

Tatiana put her coat on and told her mother she would be back soon. When her mother asked where she was going, Tatiana said, "Nowhere in particular. I need to work some things out. I won't be long."

Tatiana stepped into the cold Russian air, slipping on her hat and gloves as she began to walk. She scanned the streets, being careful to stay aware of her environment. She didn't want to be caught off guard if her mystery man appeared, but caught off guard she was when, in rounding a corner, she heard a man's voice.

"Tatiana."

She stopped, quickly turning to see who it was.

"I mean no harm."

He didn't approach, which gave Tatiana some hope he meant what he'd said.

"Who are you?" Tatiana asked, her jittery voice betraying the nervousness she sought to control.

"My name is Dmitri."

"What business do you have with me?"

"As I wrote on the card I left you, I know you are playing Antiquity. Would you trust me enough to sit and talk for a few moments?" he said, finishing with a small smile.

Tatiana knew his smile was meant to put her at ease, but, given her history with men, she remained leery.

"It is wise of you to be careful, but I may be able to help you—and the others who are playing." His response intrigued Tatiana. "Would you consider the pastry shop a few blocks down the street?" he asked, trying to convince her once again. "There will be others there, and you can leave when you choose," he said reassuringly.

Tatiana looked about to see if anyone was approaching; she focused again on Dmitri.

"The pastry shop, then," Tatiana answered after a prolonged silence.

They walked forward, Tatiana keeping a safe distance from the man who called himself "Dmitri." The shop was one of Tatiana's favorites, but it was expensive, so she was rarely a patron. They entered and looked to see if there were any open tables. The store was warm and inviting. Black-walnut paneling dressed the walls, and the irresistible scents of gingerbread and cinnamon hung in the air. Dmitri pointed to a table; it was somewhat private, yet not too far from the other customers. Tatiana nodded, and they walked to the table, hanging their coats on brass hooks mounted to the well-seasoned paneling. When the server came to take their order, Dmitri encouraged Tatiana to pick whatever she wanted. He let her know he was happy to pay. She knew she shouldn't accept his generosity, but the delicacies were so alluring she decided to accept.

Tatiana ordered an apple pastry with tea. Dmitri ordered a Napoleon cake and chose coffee with cream. While they waited for their order to arrive, Dmitri talked about the cold Russian weather and the beauty of the terrain, and explained he was also Russian, though born in a region far from Tatiana's home. When they were served, his conversation changed from chit-chat to Antiquity.

"I was a player," Dmitri said, sipping his coffee. "Once you have played, you can detect the changes. I was able to see what happened to the Space Station and what Solon did to reverse the destruction. Those who haven't played aren't able to remember what was before. When your time with Antiquity is over, you will also be able to see when history is remade," he added.

"You were a player?"

"Yes, in the ancient year of 1999. I played when the internet was just beginning to take on the world, but Antiquity predates computers. Those of us who have tried to understand Antiquity have learned it has appeared for thousands of years. We found scrolls and books that indicate history was altered well before computers were ever invented. We don't know why, but every few years Antiquity materializes. Some of my player comrades feel it is a test for mankind—to see if those who have good in their hearts can prevail over those who let evil guide their decisions. I haven't determined its purpose, but I do know how serious it can become," he said, sampling another taste of cake.

"How did you know I was a player?"

"I found you by luck, really. The mother you helped—I knew her and her family. She wasn't expected to live. Besides, old players still see notices, so I saw you used a turn for her and a turn for your sister. I read about your sister's accident, so I was able to put it all together."

"Do you know why Sage is committing these crimes? What is his motivation?"

"I do not know. I wish I could say good has always prevailed, but there have been times when those with hate in their souls and hearts have swayed things to suit their ends. I am sure you were taught about the failed assassination attempt on Hitler. It didn't fail. The event was changed by an Antiquity player allowing Hitler to survive. Still, with what I have learned, good has triumphed more times than not, so perhaps mankind has a chance."

Tatiana sat quietly at first, letting everything he said soak in. She started to open her mouth, but Dmitri held up his hand to stop her.

"There are several things I want to tell you. Someone is hunting players. I suspect a previous player is helping in the hunt. I believe that player, or someone else, wants to use current players to change history to suit his or her needs.

"There is some advice I can give you about playing. We have found that, if you take two turns quickly, Antiquity has a hard time reversing them. We aren't sure why, but Antiquity has trouble reversing compounded historical events. Antiquity will try, and it will cost you turns, but rarely will both events be set completely right. Beside this, the game cannot change things that occurred in the distant past. What I mean to say is you couldn't change Chernobyl or save the *Titanic*. It is too much for Antiquity. It can reach back a few years, maybe eight, depending on the magnitude of the history you are trying to change.

"Sometimes players don't use all of their turns, and a waiting game, a stalemate of sorts, ensues, which can go on for years, each player waiting for the other to play. This may be further motivation for whoever is hunting players. They may want to throw things off balance. If you trust the players working with you, then you may have a chance."

Dmitri stopped talking and waved to the server to freshen his cup.

It seemed as if Dmitri had talked for hours. Tatiana no longer knew what to ask. Her mind was cluttered with what Dmitri had imparted.

"Can I reach you if I need your help?" Tatiana asked.

"No, I don't give out personal information, especially given the current situation. Don't worry, though. I will be watching, and, if there is a reason we need to meet, I will find you."

After sitting for a moment in silence, Dmitri stood and helped Tatiana with her coat. He moved toward her as if to embrace, but she pulled away. He briefly smiled before walking to the counter to pay their tab. He looked at her once more before leaving the shop. Tatiana slowly made her way to the door. When she stepped onto the frozen street, she looked in each direction, but Dmitri had left no trace.

Tatiana arrived home, head spinning. She went straight to her room, intent on communicating her experience with Jeffery and Yoko. She also wanted to know what Jeffery was considering when he said he was thinking of "another way."

Tatiana opened the last email in the chain, clicked Reply All, and started typing. After sending her thoughts, Tatiana put on a sweater and walked to the kitchen to see if her mother needed help preparing the evening meal.

CHAPTER 19

PLAYER SAGE HAS BEEN PENALIZED ONE TURN. *It has been determined player Sage sent a computer device that destroyed Player Solon's computer. The destruction of Player Solon's computer and the direct attempt on his life expressly violate the rules (described in FAQ).*

Sage picked up a book and threw it against the wall. His mother came to the door and asked what had happened.

"I dropped a book."

"You haven't been yourself, son. What can I do to help?"

"I'm still upset about my cousin. I'm fine. Please go back to what you were doing," he said, turning back to his computer.

Sage no longer considered which of the three other players was responsible for interfering with his objectives. In his mind, all were against him, and he intended to act accordingly.

"That bitch's boyfriend . . . Ren?" he said aloud.

He searched and learned it was a name commonly used in Japan. *Perhaps, if I can hit them hard enough and fast enough, they won't be able to reverse the damage,* he thought as he stared at the screen.

Sage set upon his task of finding a set of appropriate historical events. It would take time, but time spent planning could yield rewards.

Though Sage didn't realize it, his approach was exactly what Dmitri stated when talking to Tatiana—Antiquity can't effectively reverse a historical change after another change has been layered on top.

CHaPTeR 20

TATIANA AND YOKO,

Players are being hunted? So now we have more than one insane somebody after us. Awesome.

This might sound crazy, but I think we should stop playing defense and start playing offense. We've been sitting, just waiting for Sage to make his next move, hoping we'll be able to undo the next terrible thing he does. You know Sage is planning something right now.

Why not change something for the better, knowing Sage would hate it? I don't think Sage will stand for it. My bet is he'll burn turns trying to reverse what we do. And if we change two things, one right after the other, like Dmitri told Tatiana, Antiquity won't be able to put things back the way they were. What do you think?

Jeffery

CHAPTER 21

AFTER READING JEFFERY'S EMAIL, Tatiana stepped out to stretch her legs. The fresh snow swirled about her as she quickened her pace. The cold air burned the back of her throat, and each time she exhaled, her breath turned into steamy wisps that vanished as quickly as they formed. She was accustomed to the cold, having lived with it all her life, but it still took her a few minutes of hard walking to get acclimated.

She hadn't considered Jeffery's approach—to go on the offensive. It was high risk. If Sage didn't take the bait and attempt to reverse what history they had affected, he would be in a position to cause havoc, and they could do little to stop him. Still, Sage had to be planning something extraordinary, and waiting and hoping they could fix what he destroyed felt like a losing proposition. Besides all that, the turns they were planning to take might truly do some good.

Normally Tatiana avoided risk, but something told her this was best. She walked past the pastry shop where she'd shared a table with Dmitri days before. She wondered what he would think of the plan Jeffery was suggesting.

What did Yoko think of the scheme? She walked on, trying to view things from all angles. As with much in life, it was difficult to come to one, clear answer, but as she rounded the corner for home, she convinced herself that Jeffery's approach was the only one that had a chance.

Tatiana opened the door, saw her mother, and smiled. Her mother was tending to dinner, and the house smelled of rich stew and warm bread. Tatiana removed her coat, walked to the kitchen, and embraced her mother. Her mom smiled, and Tatiana walked to her room. She sat in front of her computer and wrote an email to Jeffery and Yoko. When she was finished, she began searching, like Jeffery, looking for historical events that might suit their plans. From the other room, she heard her mother's call to dinner—history could wait—at least for a few minutes.

CHaPTeR 22

YOKO'S MOTHER SHOWED STEADY IMPROVEMENT despite the difficult battle with pneumonia—although it was no picnic, it wasn't cancer, and she would survive. Yoko gazed at the mountains through the window. Days ago, she'd forgotten how to appreciate their splendor. On that tear-filled day, she'd seen them as silent, soulless masses. Now they looked alive, as if they could impart wisdom, if only she knew how to speak their language. Like Jeffery and Tatiana, Yoko looked at life with renewed purpose, although she knew it shouldn't require Antiquity to understand life was a blessing.

Yoko read her email. She was thinking intently about the choices they faced and had come to the same conclusion as Tatiana. Yoko hated being "backed into a corner," but nothing she was now considering freed them from that position. Yoko expressed her concerns but ultimately agreed they should tread the path Jeffery prescribed. She, too, began searching for a piece of history, a pair of events that, if changed, would compel Sage to act.

Yoko went to the kitchen and juiced a half-dozen oranges. The scent of sweet citrus filled the air as she worked. She poured the golden-orange fluid into a tall glass and walked to her mother's room. Yoko had been delivering fresh juice every day as part of her effort to help her mother heal.

Sage abandoned food and sleep to pursue his objective, but the intensity with which he searched yielded two events of interest. Between 2016 and today, terrorist attacks had been thwarted in the United States.

In Japan, he found an event that occurred before an earthquake in Kumamoto. A year prior to the quake, a building inspector refused to allow construction on a residential tower to continue because he found irregularities in the steel members. The inspector faced immense pressure to grant waiver to the developers and the construction firm erecting the structure, but he refused and forced the companies involved to completely replace the steel at a cost of hundreds of thousands of yen. The inspector in question was subsequently given desk work and not seen again. But the building survived the quake intact, as opposed to several other buildings of similar age that suffered severe damage and cost lives. The press resurrected the stories and heaped praise upon the inspector who'd stood his ground. Sage would attempt to change the outcome to see if he could exact a greater price from Japan.

As far as the United States was concerned, Sage determined one of the terrorists' targets was a utility serving the eastern seaboard. Had the attack been successful, American lives would have been lost, and the disruption to the grid would have been substantial.

Sage intended to use Antiquity to alter both events.

CHAPTER 23

WOULD SAGE USE TURNS TO REVERSE *what we changed?
We were gambling. If he didn't, we would be in a deep hole.*

Between us, we made a list of events holding possibility. We weren't FBI profilers, we didn't know what part of the world Sage was from, and we didn't know what motivated him. We knew only what we'd seen through Antiquity—he had no problem committing murder.

Unfortunately, there were too many choices. Our list included a terrorist attack in Nice, a terrorist attack in Barcelona, a terrorist attack in Berlin, a terrorist attack in London, and a terrorist attack in New York.

On July 14, 2016, Mohamed Lahouaiej-Bouhel drove a cargo truck into a throng of partygoers celebrating Bastille Day in Nice, France, killing 86 and injuring 458. The murderer was killed by police in a gunfight.

On August 17, 2017, Younes Abouyaaqoub drove a van into a group in Barcelona, Spain, killing 13, with another passing days later; at least 130 were injured. The murderer fled and killed another as he was stealing a car. Several other incidents occurred in Spain on or about that day, and all were thought to be part of a jihadist effort. Multiple terrorists died, including Abouyaaqoub.

On December 19, 2016, Anis Amri drove a stolen truck into a group shopping at a Christmas market in Berlin, Germany; 12 were killed and 56 injured. The original driver of the truck was also found murdered. Amri was later killed in a shootout with police.

On March 22, 2017, Khalid Masood drove a car into pedestrians on the Westminster Bridge, killing five and injuring 50. The murderer later killed an unarmed policeman. Khalid was finally shot and died not far from the scene of his carnage.

On October 31, 2017, Sayfullo Saipov drove a pickup truck down a bike path in New York City, killing 8 and injuring a dozen before he was shot and apprehended.

After a few email exchanges, we agreed to reverse the attack in New York, acting on a hunch that Sage would be inclined to stop anything aiding the U.S. Secondly, we chose Nice, based on the number of people killed and injured.

Yoko outlined the agreed-upon steps in a concise email.

Jeffery, Tatiana,

I'll use a turn to reverse what happened in Nice. Tatiana, as soon as you see the notification, use a turn to reverse what happened in New York.

Yoko

CHAPTER 24

SAGE CONTINUED HIS RESEARCH but found no combination of events more appealing than the two he'd originally found. By his calculations, many would die in Japan when he altered the inspector's decision.

His second choice would cause damage to America in land and spirit.

Prior to playing, Sage walked to the kitchen and took his time selecting fruits and sweets. From a high shelf, he also pulled a bottle of brandy, which he'd acquired many years ago but had never touched. Sage opened the bottle and smiled as he poured the liquid into a crystal goblet. The liquor had a beautiful red hue and emitted scents of sweet apricot. He placed his selections on a wooden tray and carried all to his room. They made a beautiful presentation, full of color and texture.

He set the laden tray on the edge of his bed and turned to computer. His mother appeared at his bedroom door, saw the tray, and smiled.

"Your tray is beautiful. Are you feeling better?"

"Yes, mother. I'm well."

"Good, son. You enjoy yourself," she said, turning to leave the room.

Sage selected a large date, savoring its distinct sweet flavor. He wiped his fingers with dampened cotton cloth and rolled forward to begin his work. He double-clicked on Antiquity's icon, and he waited as the screen came to life. The game's familiar dialog box opened, beckoning him to take a turn and change history.

Sage typed his phrasing carefully. His finger hung over the "Enter" key as he reveled in what was about to happen.

His focus was suddenly interrupted when a notice flashed onto the screen:

Player Guru has used a turn to reverse the 2016 terrorist attack in Nice.

Sage's index finger retracted and joined the others already forming a fist.

Sage slammed his fist on the desk, which toppled a pair of marble bookends. He swore loudly, which brought his mother to the door, her eyes displaying shock and fear.

"What's happened?"

"Leave me to do my work," he said sternly.

A second notice quickly followed:

Player Mystic has influenced an event to reverse Sayfullo Saipov's terrorist attack in New York City

Sage was enraged. An anger he had never loosed rose within. His instinct at that moment was to kill. He stood and walked to the tray he had so carefully prepared, grasped it by the corner, and flung it across the room. His mother stayed away when she heard the commotion. The boy she'd raised was drifting away, and she didn't know what to do to bring him back.

Sage paced incessantly, as he tried to determine what he should do next. His mind, clouded by anger and hate, was unable to find rational thought.

He decided to use turns to undo what the others had done.

He mechanically erased what he had previously keyed, typed the phrasing he thought necessary to reverse Guru's change, and pressed "Enter."

He refrained from changing Mystic's event to save turns. He slammed both fists on the table, knocking books to the floor. He stared at Antiquity's notifications before rising from his chair, donning his coat, and leaving without a word.

CHAPTER 25

TATIANA HADN'T NOTICED the black sedan parked down the street as she walked home from school that day. She was deep in thought, intent to get to her computer and Antiquity. She kicked the snow from her boots before opening the door and entering her home. As she closed the door and turned to step into the room, she was immediately restrained by someone with a vise-like grip. She struggled but was no match for whoever was holding her. She called her mother's name, but a cloth bearing the sickening smell of a strong medicine covered her nose and mouth. The nausea was instantaneous, and her muscles turned to rubber. She longed for a breath of cold, fresh air before all went black.

She fought for consciousness but managed only momentary glimpses. She could detect only the sensation of being jostled about.

Tatiana slowly woke from her drug-induced sleep. There was an IV in her arm; she tried reaching to remove it but found she was strapped to a gurney. She felt sick and fought the impulse to vomit. The light in the room was subdued, and she heeded her body's call for rest.

Tatiana's sleep was fraught with nightmares of Jeffery badly burned. In one, she stood in front of Jeffery's door in a poorly maintained hospital corridor. Rats scurried between sheet-covered bodies lying on floor. Suddenly she realized she was standing in the hallway of a morgue. She reached for the knob to open the door, but the rusted steel spun round and round. Pounding its hard surface, she hoped to jar it loose, but her efforts were for naught. Smoke flowed from the gap between floor and door. It twisted and curled, moving upward, clinging to the surface of the door. She tried to call for help but was unable to emit a sound.

Again Tatiana woke, her heartbeat throbbing in her ears. She couldn't discern nightmare from reality for several minutes, still reeling from the images haunting her.

A woman in nurse's garb was standing beside her, checking her pulse. Tatiana managed to ask where she was, but the woman didn't answer. Closing her eyes, Tatiana fell back into her nightmarish slumber.

She was awakened by the noise of two men arguing. As her head began to clear, she was able to discern that their argument revolved around the quantity of medication she was forced to inhale. One of the men was calling the other ". . . a fool." She quietly agreed with the man who called the other a fool. One of the men, a man of some heft, noticed Tatiana was awake and became quiet. He walked to where she was lying.

"You're awake," the man stated in a gruff voice.

"Where am I?"

"Where isn't important."

"Why am I here?"

"You are here because we need your help."

"My help?" Tatiana questioned.

"Yes, you will understand," he coolly remarked. "You need to eat something," he said as he turned to see the nurse entering the room.

The nurse returned in short order with broth and juice. Setting the tray on a small table just beyond the foot of the bed, she came back to Tatiana to remove the IV that was irritating her skin. She unbound the straps restraining Tatiana's arms and feet. It felt good to be able to move again, as her feet touched the floor, her legs still reluctant to support her. She wobbled her way to the table and sat. Although she didn't have much of an appetite, she knew she had to get something in her stomach, so she leaned over the warm liquid and slowly began eating.

The big man who had spoken earlier let her eat for some time before joining her at the table.

"My name is Aleksei. How is your soup?" he asked, not caring if she answered.

"I've had better."

"Do you know why we need your help?"

"No," Tatiana answered, not looking at him.

"Let me explain why my clients and I want your assistance. We need you and your friends to use Antiquity to help achieve, shall we say, certain outcomes. It won't be difficult," he finished, forcing a smile.

Tatiana set the spoon beside the bowl before looking at the man squarely, asking, "And if we don't want to participate?"

"You will find it best not to consider that line of thinking. It isn't productive," he said, as his false smile turned into tightly compressed lips.

"Your stay with us can be relatively comfortable and relatively short, or . . . let's not go further down that path. You are free to move around your room—but nowhere else without an escort. Rest. We will call on you soon," he said, tapping his knuckles on the table before walking away.

Tatiana's emotions were a jumble of anger, concern, fear, and worry. She was trapped and saw no path to freedom. She wondered what these people wanted with their turns. *If we cooperate, will they let me go? They'll have what they want.* The more she raced through questions, the more fear rose within her. She coached herself. *Don't panic—you'll lose if you panic.* She lay on her bed, pulled her legs to her chest, and wrapped her arms tightly round them. As she calmed down, the remnants of the drug pushed her into another fitful sleep.

Tatiana woke to the sound of Aleksei's voice.

"Get up Tatiana," he said sternly.

"How long have I been sleeping?"

"How long doesn't matter. It is time we get started with our work," he said curtly. "In your bathroom, you will find toiletries and a change of clothes. Please prepare yourself. I will return shortly."

Tatiana shuffled to the bathroom and turned on the light. The room was cold, the light harsh. She blinked and rubbed her eyes in an effort to adjust. The water refused to warm, and she shivered as she washed. When she was finished, she picked up a neatly folded towel sitting on a wire mesh shelf. The towel smelled clean, giving her some comfort. Her sister thought her crazy, but Tatiana always liked the faint smell of chlorine on linens, even when very young. The clothes they'd left her were light-blue hospital scrubs. She thought it odd, but they were comfortable.

Aleksei was standing at the center of the room and motioned for her to follow. Tatiana considered returning a gesture of another nature but refrained. He escorted her to a room filled with computers manned by people who looked as if they hadn't had a day off for weeks. She continued to follow as he walked to a desk with a vacant chair. The computer at this station was familiar—it was hers. The stickers she'd applied when she'd first received it were still partially in place but faded and torn. The man motioned her to sit, and Tatiana complied.

"The first item on the agenda is to log into Antiquity and write an email. I want to see if Antiquity's email is working properly. You can write a test email to yourself," he said, pointing to her laptop.

Tatiana grumbled, logging into Antiquity.

As she opened an email, she was abruptly pulled away from her computer. Pain shot through her arm where she'd been grabbed.

Tatiana watched as a man sat down at her laptop and composed an email. She was filled with anger as she saw the words take form. Try as she might, she couldn't free herself, and she was tired of that feeling.

Jeffery,

I need your help. I've been taken from my home. Some men want me to use my turns to help them. They need you to help them, too. I don't know what will happen to me if you can't. I don't know how to ask, Jeffery, but can you come here? I am frightened and don't know what to do. They say they will make all the arrangements. Please, Jeffery.

Tatiana

Tatiana looked at Aleksei.

"Why bring Jeffery into this?" Tatiana snarled fiercely.

The man holding her by the arm chuckled, taking pleasure in her frustration.

"We have plans and need both of you here."

Though it made no difference, she drifted for a moment, wondering how a choice to download a game had led to where she now stood. The man holding her tightened his grip. His hand made her skin crawl. She knew they wouldn't stop until they had what they wanted.

"I have matters to tend to. When I return, I will expect you and Jeffery to contribute to our mission," he said, nodding to the man holding Tatiana.

Aleksei walked away, saying nothing more.

CHAPTER 26

SAGE RETURNED FROM HIS WALK with a clearer head, though still simmering. He nodded to his mother as he passed. The mess he'd made had been cleaned. He didn't consider thanking his mother. *Women are supposed to clean,* he rationalized. He sat in front of his computer and signed in. A notification was open and centered on Antiquity's screen:

Sage reviewed Antiquity's tally:

Turns Taken		Penalties	Turns Remaining
Solon	3	1	3
Mystic	4	1	2
Guru	4	1	2
Sage	3	2	2

He was disgusted. "Mother, mother, are you there?" he called as he walked toward the kitchen.

CHAPTER 27

I RETURNED HOME, threw down my things, and logged on.

Reversing Yoko's event had cost Sage a penalty and a turn, but there was no notice of reversing Tatiana's change.

"Better than nothing."

A new email from Tatiana was waiting. I quickly opened and read the new arrival.

"Shit!"

I read it again, hoping that, the first time through, I'd missed something; the second reading made things no better. My mind began racing.

I had to do something, but what? Travel to Russia to help a girl I hardly knew? Get myself killed or locked up in a gulag?

"Shit."

I wanted to lock the door to my room and forget I'd ever heard of Antiquity. I wanted life to get back to normal. This wasn't me. *I'm not some Harry Potter getting ready to duel with Voldemort and save the world.*

They'll let her go if I don't respond. She'll understand. My play-it-safe voice was winning. Another voice barked how Tatiana and Yoko had hunted me down to save my life. I can't curl up in my room and let this happen. My stomach tightened.

I thought, *Maybe I can use Antiquity to free her* but reconsidered, figuring they would just go after her again, and, eventually my turns would be gone.

I opened my desk drawer. I dug through some piled-up school crap until I found it—my passport. I threw it back into my drawer and picked up my phone.

"Wha's up, dude?" Jason answered.

"I think I'm about to do something stupid crazy."

"Don't even ask Susie out. She'll spit in your face," which didn't do much for my ego.

"Thanks. That helps. That's not what I'm talking about. If my parents call you in a couple of days asking where I am, I need you to tell them I went to a tech show with friends."

"So you want me to lie to your parents?"

"I know it's a shitty thing to ask, but it's important."

"Tell me what the hell this is about, or I'm not covering for your ass."

"It's about a girl, but it's more than that. Some people kidnapped her, and she needs my help. It's hard to explain."

"Wait—did I just hear you right? Somebody took some chick, and you're going to play Superman and save her? Have you lost your f'n mind? Call the police. What are you thinkin'? How do you know this woman?" His voice was getting higher.

"I can't tell you the whole story, but it started with this game . . . " He cut me off before I could finish.

"No way! Don't you even say you met her online. Dude, you're losing it. This is some kind of setup. You'll get there, they'll chain you in the basement, torture your dumb ass, cut you up, and bury you in their vegetable garden. You can't do this. Have you ever met this girl in person? She's probably some pedophile sickie actin' like a chick!"

"I know it sounds bad—and you know me. You know I hate taking risks. But this is different. This is the real deal. I can't let these people hurt her. They want something from me, something about the game, something really serious. I keep calling it 'a game,' but it isn't a game. It can cause some major world shit to go down. I'm not on a suicide mission. Dude, I promise—I will make it back and tell you the whole tale. Just cover for me . . . please."

"Where the hell is she?" he asked in a calmer tone.

"I can't say. I don't want you to have to lie about anything else. Just cover me for a couple of days; after that, you can tell my parents I made you lie for me. Deal?"

"Dude, if you die, I'm going to make sure they write "Stupid" on your tombstone. Two days, no more—and you'd better text me that it's all cool, or I'll kick your ass," he said reluctantly.

"Thanks. I'll let you know what's happening as soon as I can. And thanks again. I owe you."

"Yeah, yeah. Shut up, and f'n be careful."

He hung up.

I opened an email and typed a response.

Tatiana,
Tell whoever is holding you that I will come. Tell them to make whatever arrangements they need to so I can get there. Don't be afraid. I'll help. I don't care about my turns.
Jeffery

I opened my desk drawer and again pulled out my passport. I knew I should tell my folks what was happening, but I also knew they wouldn't let me go. I was going. I didn't know where this would lead, but Tatiana needed me, and I was going. I started pulling clothes out of my closet. I was moving quickly. I wanted to get everything together before my parents showed up and started asking questions.

I should write Yoko and let her know what is happening. I reconsidered. I didn't want to drag her into it, but I did owe her an email. I wrote a short one, telling her I had to travel with my mom and dad for a couple of days and that she didn't need to worry. I also wrote that Tatiana's sister posted a message on her Facebook page saying her family had to travel to see a very sick cousin and that they'd left unexpectedly. *Yoko's smart. She'll figure something is bogus after a few days, but this might buy some time.* I hated lying, but this might keep her safe, at least for a little while.

As I stood, another email arrived. It was Tatiana. I read it from where I stood.

Jeffery,
Thank you so much for helping me. The man who is directing things said to call the number at the bottom

of this email when you are ready. A driver will come for you. He said the driver will have a ticket and will give you money to travel. The driver will make sure you get on the plane. Be careful.

404 893 5235

Tatiana

I wrote mom and dad a note. I didn't know what to say, so I just wrote that I was sorry I hadn't told them, but I'd gotten invited by some friends to travel to a computer show. I said I would be back in a few days, telling another lie.

I called the number, and a man told me to remove my hard drive and bring it with me. He said he was coming to pick me up at the house, but I told him he needed to pick me up at my school. I told him mom or dad would get home before he got to the house. He agreed. I stowed the hard drive in my coat pocket, grabbed my over-stuffed backpack, and headed out the front door. I wondered if I would ever see home again.

A black sedan pulled up to the walk. A large, grim-looking man got out of the car, leaving the vehicle running. I felt like I was in a movie, but there was no one to yell, "Cut!" when the scene was over. He opened the rear door and asked that I hand over my backpack. He tossed it on the rear seat and turned to face me.

"Did you bring the hard drive?" he asked in a low, gravelly tone.

I carefully pulled it out of my coat pocket to show him.

"Good. On the way to the airport, you can pack it for shipping. There are packing materials on the front seat. Do you have your passport?" he asked.

"Yes."

"Good. Get in. It's time to go," he rumbled as he slammed the rear door and walked back to the driver's side.

I got in and closed the door. The reality of the situation began to sink in.

On our way to the airport, he gave me advice on how to wrap the drive. He told me how things would unfold once at the airport. He would do the talking, posing as a family member who was helping to get me on my way. He pulled two envelopes out of his inside overcoat pocket. One contained a ticket and the other cash.

"Don't lose your ticket, and don't spend the money foolishly," he said, looking briefly at me and then back at the road.

As he walked me through each instruction, I nodded, only half paying attention. I had questions but decided not to ask.

All went as expected at the airport. Before I boarded, he went over my itinerary and my connecting flights, and he told me I was to ask airline personnel to make certain I got to the proper gates. As he was finishing his instructions, an announcement echoed from the overhead speakers. It was my flight. It was time to board. He said, "Go" and told me once again to focus on what he had directed.

"Journey well," he said, pointing toward the door that led to the plane. I had maintained a remarkably even temperament, but I was starting to freak. I wanted to turn and sprint for home. After handing the attendant my ticket, I walked down the gray-carpeted corridor to the plane. I arrived at the door, and, after a few minutes' waiting, I was in my seat, my backpack stowed overhead. The plane was only partially full, and its door was pulled closed with a loud latching sound. It wasn't long before the silver machine lurched away from the gate and started its slow roll toward the runway. After a brief announcement from the captain saying we were cleared, the engines roared, and we accelerated. The tires thudded at each concrete joint, and I gripped down hard on the armrests. The last mechanical noise I heard before closing my eyes was the landing gear finding its home for the flight ahead.

I changed planes in New York and was on my way to Frankfurt, Germany. The attendants fed us, and, despite the countless unknowns I would be facing, I dozed during the eight-hour flight. Germany was dark and cold, but my final destination would be much more so. There was an agonizing two-hour layover in Germany, and my folks were texting me constantly. I was forced to continue embellishing my original story, and I could tell they were angry and didn't believe me. Finally, the airport's speakers came alive with the news that my flight was boarding. I followed the rest of the passengers onto the plane that would take me to my destination—Lensk, Russia. I was tired, and the flight was long. We landed on a snow-covered airstrip in the dead of night. We disembarked via a portable stairway into the bitter-cold, snow-laden air that stung my face each time the wind gusted. I had never experienced cold like this, and it stole my breath. I hurried toward a building a football field away. I didn't know what I would find there, but knew I wanted to get out of the Lensk weather.

Walking through the door, I found myself in a storage area. The few others arriving with me walked methodically up the stairs that I assumed led to the terminal. I followed. As I neared the top of the steps, I saw a man wearing a black coat with a fur-lined collar. I looked to my left and right and back at him, and he was still staring at me. When I crested the top stair, I stood still. Two of the remaining passengers rubbed past me and rendezvoused with people who were glad to see them. I wished I were standing in their shoes. The man with whom I had locked eyes put his hands in his pockets and walked toward me.

"Jeffery?" he said in an amplified voice as he continued moving in my direction. "Welcome to Russia. How was your trip? No problems? Here—let me take your bag," he said, reaching for my backpack.

I twisted slightly, indicating I didn't need help.

"Where is Tatiana?" I asked before we took a step.

"I will take you to her," he responded, pulling back his hand.

I walked at his side through the terminal and back into the frigid Lensk night. We got into his vehicle and sped into the Russian blackness.

CHAPTER 28

RATHER THAN IMMEDIATELY USING his final turns, as he'd planned, Sage decided to take a more conservative approach. He wanted to see what the other players would do. Ironically, Sage had traded places with the others. They had taken his offensive approach, and he was shifting to a defensive mindset, hoping he would be the last player to have turns.

Sage also felt he could seek retribution outside the confines of Antiquity. If he could get to Jeffery, he could find the others. He believed he could still be the last standing.

CHAPTER 29

FIVE MILES OR SO INTO THE JOURNEY, the man driving mumbled that we had to stop for petrol and told me to stay put. It was a lonely outpost—only three pumps and one of them said керосин. Under that verbiage was a partially faded word, "ker se e." I allowed it to occupy my mind for a few minutes while the man was pumping gas. *Kerosene*, I concluded. Maybe an odd time to play a word game.

After fueling up, my driver opened the trunk and banged around looking for something. He slammed the lid closed and slid back into the car, which, by that point, had lost the precious little heat it had produced getting us this far. He turned to me and held out a stocking cap.

"Pull this over your eyes, and don't take it off until I say. Understand?" he demanded in a voice he hadn't used until now.

"Yeah—I understand."

I took it from his hand. I pulled the itchy woolen cap over my face and said nothing else. After two tries, the car rumbled to life, and we once again started to move through the frozen Russian terrain.

For the first few miles, we drove without making a turn. The cap over my head was killing me. I wanted to rip it off and scratch every inch of my head. About the time I was ready to ask if I could remove it, the car turned abruptly, and I found myself up against the car's side window. After several more twists and turns, we crossed over what felt like railroad tracks. We drove another quarter mile or so and pulled to a stop. The car went silent, except for the ticking sound of the hot engine. My driver got out on his side and came to mine. He grabbed my backpack from the rear seat, opened my door, and helped me out of the car. I was unsteady, with the woolen blindfold still covering my eyes, and tripped several times as he moved me along.

He pulled me backward to a stop after climbing a short flight of stairs. He pounded on the surface, and, before long, I could hear a bolt sliding behind what I now assumed was a door. It opened, and the two had a short conversation in what sounded like Russian. Then he began pulling me along again. Light was filtering through my prickly cap. We stopped again, and he removed the cap. The relief was like having a bad tooth removed, and I rubbed my face and head with satisfaction. My driver led me to a room, opened the door, and turned on the lights. He unzipped my backpack and searched it, throwing my clothes on the floor. He didn't bother to repack it when finished.

"Wait here. Someone will be coming to talk with you," he announced before turning to leave.

"Hey, where is Tatiana?"

He left the room, closing the door behind him without answering my question.

Like the captive man does in every movie, I walked to the door and tried the knob . . . locked. I looked around the room. There was nothing to speak of in the room—no furniture, no bathroom, only walls, ceiling, floor. The walls and floor were gray cement. There was no vent cover that could be removed to let me crawl through the ducts to Tatiana and then to freedom. The ceiling was at least twelve feet high. It was a dropped ceiling, and there was a chance I could pop a tile to get a look, but there was no ladder to aid. I was beat, and I decided to take a power nap while I was waiting for that someone to come back to my room. I lay down on the cold floor and used my backpack for a pillow. I closed my eyes.

I didn't hear the door open. I was being shaken, and the jostling was accompanied by a male voice.

"Jeffery . . . Jeffery, wake up. You've been asleep for some time now."

I opened my eyes. It wasn't my driver, but another man, this one rounder than my driver. It took me a moment to focus.

"I've ordered a meal. Eat, and then we'll get started."

"Where is Tatiana? I want to see that she's alright," I asked, figuring if I kept asking, I might eventually get a straight answer.

"Eat, and then I will take you to her."

I didn't believe him.

A woman in scrubs entered the room with a tray. On it was a bowlful of what looked like stew, a chunk of crusty bread, and a bottle of milk. The stew smelled good, and I didn't know when I would get a chance to eat again, so I indulged.

Yoko read Jeffery's email and was left with a troubled feeling that wouldn't' fade. Yoko was perceptive and trusted her intuition. She knew something was wrong, but she didn't know how to figure out the wrong. Jeffery was traveling, and so was Tatiana; neither would be in a position to correspond for several days.

She wondered if Jeffery and Tatiana's trips were related. How could she find out more from what seemed a million miles away? She sat in her room, and, for the first time in weeks, she felt utterly alone.

CHAPTER 30

"COME WITH ME, JEFFERY," he said curtly.

"Let's do this," I said, trying to sound like I had some control over the situation. He waited for me just outside the door, closing it after me. He trailed slightly as we walked down the bright corridor.

"This way."

We walked toward a set of double doors. The soles of the big man's shoes made a loud *clip-clop* sound that echoed off of the hard surfaces. We reached the doors, and he pushed open one of the two and held it so I could walk through.

We entered a busy room, full of people using computers. Exposed cables and power cords hung from an open ceiling. He led me to an open desk and explained my hard drive had arrived and had been installed in the tower sitting under the desk. I moved the mouse, and, when the screen came to life, I could see Antiquity was up, waiting for a password. He then tapped the shoulder of the girl sitting in the chair beside us. She turned and looked at me.

"Jeffery," she said in English with a perfect hint of her native accent. "I'm sorry. They tricked me. I didn't want to involve you."

She rose, and, as she stepped back, I could see her eyes had turned watery. When I looked at the girl who was standing before me, I lost all perspective. She suddenly seemed to be the only one in the room. Her tear-filled eyes seemed to magnify the depth of their blue. Her cheekbones were high and cast beautiful, haunting shadows on her delicate white skin that boasted only a few light-red freckles. She had tied up her strawberry-blond hair, but some unruly strands formed soft wisps around the sides of her face and neck. She was tall and thin, and I could tell by the darkness beneath her eyes that sleep had been difficult to come by. Still, she fought her emotions and forced a smile. Her scarlet-red lips needed no aid from lipstick. I couldn't stop looking. I had imagined what Tatiana looked like when we were exchanging emails, but my imaginings didn't do her justice. She was striking. The big man destroyed the moment with a grumble, and my brain started functioning again.

"Don't worry, Tatiana." I smiled.

The big man asked that we follow. As we walked away, I scanned the room, hoping I would see something, some vulnerability that might open an avenue of escape. He took us to a dimly lit conference room and directed us to sit. Tatiana and I each reached for the same chair, and our hands met. I flinched, pulling away, and gave an awkward apology. I slid to my left and pulled out the next chair, letting Tatiana have the first.

A door opened on the opposite side of the room. Three figures entered and sat at the far end of the large table. It was so dark, I couldn't make out any of the faces shrouded in shadow. A man began speaking in what sounded like Russian to me, but, when I looked at Tatiana, I could see she didn't understand the language, either—maybe a different dialect. As he stopped, another man spoke in English—I assumed he was translating.

"These people you see working, they are looking for opportunities," the translator finished. Then the first man began speaking again. "They are looking at scenarios that, if altered, would benefit us. After we analyze which scenarios have the highest probability of achieving our ends, we will choose one. That's where you become important. You will use Antiquity turns to complete the process. There may be unanticipated results that would require you to use another turn to, shall we say, make adjustments. If you cooperate, there will be no problems. If you decide to fight our efforts, you or a member of your family will face harm." The translator stopped.

"What are you trying to achieve?" I asked, breaking the silence.

The translator went from English to whatever, and there was silence for a moment. The man in the shadows spoke again.

"The same thing men have always wanted—wealth and power," the translator said, without a smile.

The man covered in darkness spoke briefly once more.

"We will soon require your assistance," the translator said and followed the others out of the room.

Tatiana looked at me.

"What should we do?" she asked, wishing there was a solution she hadn't considered.

"I don't know if we'll have a choice. We need to think of some way to get out of here and, if we can, cause them some major-league trouble." I dropped to a whisper as our chaperone entered the room.

"I need you to email each other through Antiquity to make certain the game is working properly," he instructed.

We tested Antiquity's email application, and it worked as it always had. "Good," he grunted.

He walked us to the building's cafeteria.

"If we detect for one moment you aren't following our rules, life will become very difficult. Do you understand?" he said, demanding an answer.

"Yes," we answered simultaneously.

"If you are still hungry, you can get something," he said pushing open the door to the cafeteria.

I looked at Tatiana and shrugged. We entered the room and walked to the beginning of the food line. I had just eaten, but I was still hungry.

"He didn't explain the rules, and I'm surprised he's left us alone," I stated quietly, handing Tatiana a tray.

"I doubt they'll leave us alone. I don't think those men standing against the wall are waiting on a meal," she said with a small grin. I smiled, trying to avoid their gaze.

"Do you know what language those men were speaking?" I asked as we stood looking at the steaming food behind the glass guards.

"No. I could understand only one out of ten words. I didn't recognize the dialect."

The options weren't appealing, but we picked our poisons, and women wearing neat blue aprons plated our choices. We found seats at a table as far away from our observers as possible. The scene was surreal. Just hours ago, I was in Virginia, emailing Tatiana, and now I was sitting next to her. I looked at her as she poked at the food on her tray. She glanced up and caught me staring. My skin went hot, and I knew my cheeks were turning red. I turned away in embarrassment.

"Do you have any ideas?" she asked.

One of the men who had been at the wall was walking toward our table. We put our heads down and focused on eating, hoping he would pass by. Instead, he sat at our table and looked at us. Tatiana spoke to the man in Russian, and he returned a comment.

"He said he is just here to visit," Tatiana smiled insincerely as she looked back at our new companion.

We shared a silent meal with the exception of six words spoken; *please pass the salt* and *thank you*. We finished our meals, cleared the table, and returned the trays.

As we approached the exit, another man standing along the wall intersected our path and told us to wait. After ten minutes or so, our original escort arrived and took us to a room that was constructed of steel and reinforced glass on three sides. It was a fishbowl. Another man was waiting beside the room's only entry door.

Through the panes, I could see several cots and a bathroom against the back wall. My backpack was sitting on one of the cots.

"This is where you'll sleep," he said bluntly and opened the door.

We walked into the room. The door slammed, and I jumped. Tatiana quietly laughed, but I felt like a goof. The bathroom was stark but had the essentials—toilet paper, a couple of towels, two toothbrushes.

"Has this been your room?" I asked Tatiana.

"Yes, it could be worse."

"I need to use the bathroom."

"Yes, please," she said, amused that I'd announced it.

Tatiana was sitting Indian style on her cot when I emerged.

"Better?"

"Better," I said, smiling.

I walked to the cot beside Tatiana's and sat down.

"It's extremely bright. How can you sleep?" I questioned.

"They'll turn off the lights soon."

I stretched out and heard a clicking noise, and, suddenly, most of the lights dropped out. Blackness gave way to tones of sepia, and, in the dim light, I could see Tatiana had also lain down.

"Do you think they're listening to us?"

"It's Russia, Jeffery. Someone is always listening.

"I didn't think you would come," she said softly.

"I didn't think I would, either. I would be lying if I said I came without hesitation. I almost decided not to."

"So, why did you?"

I took some time to gather my thoughts.

"Two reasons, I guess. I couldn't turn my back on you, and I'm sick of always playing it safe. I've been telling myself that one day I'll make a difference, saying I'll step out of the shadows and take a chance in life, but I never do. I'm tired of living that way, so I went against every one of my instincts. I about panicked when I was walking up to the gate to board the plane. I hate the feeling of being afraid. Sometimes I think I'm the only one on the planet who feels like I do." I stopped, thinking I should shut up.

Tatiana didn't say anything for a while, and I figured she hadn't liked what I said.

"I think you're brave. I'm also tired of living the way I do," she said, sounding like she wanted to say more.

She went silent again. I thought she had fallen asleep, but then she began talking.

"My father left us when I was nine. He wasn't much of a father; he didn't treat us well. Because of him, I don't trust people, especially men. What I hate is I still want him to be proud of me. When I get a good grade or sing in the chorus, I wish I could tell him. One time, when I was in a play at school, I thought I saw him in the audience. I looked for him long after everyone was gone. I never found him. I don't think he was ever there. I wanted to believe he was." She grew quiet again.

"Shit, Tatiana. That's messed up. I wish I knew what to say, but I'm not that smart. Look, I don't know what's going to happen to either of us, but I fought my fears, and I'm here. I don't know if I'll be able to every time, but I'm not giving up. You're not denying anything. You know what's going on; like me, you just need to keep trying. I think I can change. Why not you?" I stopped talking because I figured I was starting to sound pretty dumb.

"You're smarter than you think. Goodnight, Jeffery," she said as she pulled up her covers.

"Goodnight," I said, doing the same.

———

"I don't want them in the same room, you idiot," Aleksei slammed his fist on the table.

"You said you wanted them to feel comfortable. There're a couple of kids telling each other their heartbreak stories. What does it matter? Maybe they'll come to our side," one of the men murmured.

"You heard me. I don't trust them. They may cause a disruption that would interfere with my plans. I want them separated." Aleksei got up from his chair and deliberately let it roll. It slammed against the wall as he was walking out of the room.

Early the following morning, we were jarred awake.

"Both of you—pick up your things. We are moving you," the man commanded.

"What?" I asked, half asleep.

"The boss wants you moved to separate rooms. Let's go."

I turned toward Tatiana, our eyes meeting. I wondered if she could see my disappointment. We followed him down the corridor, stopping first at Tatiana's room.

"Drop off your things," he said, opening the door.

She did as asked, and we walked to my room. He opened the door and said the same to me.

"I'll take you to the cafeteria."

Before walking away from the serving line, I grabbed a small pile of clean napkins, and slid them into my pocket. It occurred to me that a napkin could be used to pass a message. As before, a guard sat at our table while we ate. When we were finished, we were escorted to our rooms. I said "Goodbye" to Tatiana when we stopped at her door. I hesitated before walking away, and she seemed in no hurry to part. She returned a "Goodbye" when our guide grew impatient. We were three doors apart.

As we walked to my room, I noticed a man in what appeared to be a maintenance closet. There were paint cans and solvents. Dad stored similar cans full of paint thinner, acetone, and lacquer thinner in his garage. The big man said nothing when we reached my room. His silence was more blessing than insult, and I stepped inside. Flopping down on the bed, I began thinking. I started by praying for a miracle. I had to come up with a plan and needed all the help I could get. I wanted to text mom and dad to give them some sense of comfort, but the Russian bastards holding us had confiscated my phone.

I was down to pen and napkins. I was surprised they didn't take my pens when they'd riffled through my backpack looking for contraband. Certainly James Bond could make a missile from a pen; I was going to put it to conventional use.

I wrote:

Test message

I refolded the napkin and examined it to see if the ink bled through—it was clean. I stowed the pen and put the napkin in my pocket.

Jeffery's mother and father were well beyond worried. Jeffery had his rebellious moments, but he had never done anything like this.

They called Jason, and he confirmed Jeffery's story, however, not one of Jeffery's other friends knew anything about a show. His parents called teachers and the administrative staff, and none knew his whereabouts. The next call was to the police. Missing teenagers weren't an unusual occurrence, but they sent an officer to conduct an interview.

When he was finished, the officer indicated he would follow the department's protocol and tried to reassure them it would be alright. His statement provided no comfort. They knew something was wrong and intended to take further steps.

Jeffery's father knew a senator and reached out. The senator said he would try a few avenues that the police wouldn't. Next, Jeffery's father initiated a search for a private investigator.

CHAPTER 31

THE MORE THOUGHT YOKO GAVE to what Jeffery had said in his email, the more she suspected Jeffery and Tatiana were in trouble. She searched Facebook and was unable to find any "Smirnov" page remotely matching a profile for Tatiana's sister. She decided she would try to contact Tatiana's mother. It took some digging, but Yoko located a number. Making the call from her parents' landline, she dialed, and there were several delays and clicks before the call connected. After a few rings, a woman answered, speaking in Russian. Yoko asked a question in English.

"No understand. Call back," the woman said in a heavy accent before hanging up the phone.

Yoko sat on the edge of her bed. *The woman who answered didn't understand English, yet she asked that I call back. She knows someone who understands English,* Yoko concluded. *How long to wait? Is it a neighbor, Tatiana's sister, a priest, a delivery man? She may mean call tomorrow or the next day.* Yoko waited twenty minutes. If the same woman answered, Yoko hoped to communicate a few more words.

"Allo," a different voice answered.

"Is this Tatiana Smirnov's house?"

"Yes."

"May I speak to Tatiana?"

"Tatiana is not here."

"Do you know how I can reach her?"

"No, she is gone."

Yoko thought she could hear crying in the background.

"Do you know where Tatiana is?" Yoko asked, now hearing distinct weeping.

"No, I'm sorry, but I do not," the woman answered back, her voice laden with emotion.

"Tatiana is my friend, and I'm trying to find her."

Yoko could hear a chorus of crying now. She waited, and after what seemed a long silence, the woman spoke again.

"They gave my mother a drug, and, when it wore off, Tatiana was gone," she said in a tone so sad Yoko had a hard time knowing what to say next. "We asked police to help, but they are busy and . . . " Her voice trailed off. "Did you say you were a friend?"

"Yes, yes, I am," Yoko said intently, "Are you Tatiana's sister?"

"Yes, I am—Alena" she said quietly. "Can you help us find Tatiana?"

"I will try," Yoko said back. Yoko gave Alena her phone number.

"Thank you."

"Call anytime," Yoko said, trying to give some comfort.

"Thank you," she repeated.

There was an awkward silence before Yoko said her goodbye and disconnected the call.

Yoko recounted the words spoken and their desperate quality—*what to do?*

CHAPTER 32

THE RATTLE OF MY DOOR AWAKENED ME from a shallow sleep. It opened to a woman in scrubs. She said her name was Vera. She was jumping between what I presume was Russian and broken English, telling me I was to meet shortly with "the men." I sat up and looked about the room. The pace of my activity was apparently too slow, and she insisted I hurry. I nodded, swung my legs over the bed's edge, and stood.

"You, bathroom," she said tersely, as she opened the door to the hall. "I come back."

I thought of Tatiana as I looked in the mirror and wondered what she thought of me.

"Ready?" Vera's voice echoed from the other room. She had given me all of two minutes.

"Almost," I answered in a muddled voice, spitting toothpaste into the sink.

I finished, and we left the room. She led me to the now-familiar cafeteria. Vera instructed me to wait for a few moments. Tatiana was already seated. Our eyes met, and we both smiled. I joined her.

"Did Vera say we are going to another meeting?"

"Yes," Tatiana answered quietly. "Maybe they know what they need us for."

As she finished her sentence, one of the guards made his way to our table and sat down. We sat in silence. I pulled the napkin with the test message from my pocket with my opposite hand and nonchalantly slid it under Tatiana's leg. It startled her, and she looked at me. I ignored her stare, but the guard asked her something. She answered, and he seemed satisfied.

A big man entered the room and approached our table.

"Follow" was his only word.

This time, the room was well-lit. We were told to sit at the far end of the table. Soon the entertaining group from the previous day made their way into the room and sat opposite. I studied their faces as they looked at us. The translator once again took up his work. One of the men spoke, and the translator turned back as if to confirm what was said before speaking to us.

"This is Aleksei, Viktor, and Dmitri," he said, pointing to each of the men as he said their names.

Dmitri? Surely it can't be . . . I turned to look at Tatiana. The look on her face said it all. It was a look of disbelief.

The translator continued speaking. It was explained that the analysts had concluded there were three possible scenarios meeting the preferred criteria. They would shortly choose one. Once that choice was made, we would be required to use our turns to better their cause. They estimated it would take two more days to complete their work.

"Are you ready to help?" Aleksei asked in English, talking over the translator.

"I still don't understand exactly how our turns are going to help you," I asked.

"It isn't important you know the details. What is important is that you understand your role. Are you ready to assist?" the translator asked as Aleksei abandoned his English.

Neither Tatiana nor I responded to his question.

Aleksei banged the table and spoke again.

"Did you hear my question? Are you ready to assist us?" the translator said in an elevated voice, seeming to communicate Aleksei's frustration.

"Yes," I answered, and I followed with, "Of course."

Why had they drug us back in here for this? Then it occurred to me: they wanted Tatiana to see Dmitri to play with her mind—*damn.*

I asked if could let our parents know we weren't in danger and would be returning home shortly. When the translator finished expressing my questions, one of the men grunted a one-word answer that the translator quickly passed along: "Later."

They stood and walked out of the room.

Tatiana and I looked at each other after we heard the answer to my question.

"Do you think Dmitri was with them when he met with you?"

"I don't know. Why would he tell me what he did about Antiquity if he was working for them? What he told me could work against them. He's just another man who lied," Tatiana said indifferently.

"Screw it, Tatiana. Forget him. It's you and me now. We've got to get out of this prison and do whatever we can to stop them."

She turned to look at me and was about to say something when our escort came through the door.

I lay in bed thinking about what Tatiana had said—about being lied to. It had wounded her, and I found myself wanting to prove to her that there were decent guys in the world. But I wouldn't be able to prove anything if we remained captive. I remembered how dad once used his pocket knife to open our door when we were locked out of the house. If I could get out of my room, I might also be able to bust into the closet where all the paint was stored. I shouldn't have, but I'd once played around with dad's lacquer thinner and almost burned down our garage. We could cause one hell of a disruption if I could find a solvent like that.

I raised my knees and pulled up the covers. I reached for a napkin and the pen I had tucked under my mattress. I printed in as small a type as I could manage on the cafeteria parchment:

I have an idea to get out of my room.

I will say more later.

I folded the napkin, gently creased its edges, and tucked it in my pocket. Lying back, I opened my book and started to read, but my eyes glazed, and I let it fall to my chest. I hadn't slept well lately but now fell away from my stark reality.

My power nap was interrupted by the sound of a key turning my door's lock. It was Vera, come to fetch me once more.

"Lunch," she blurted matter-of-factly and motioned for me to follow. *Lunch already; I was out longer than I thought.* I pointed toward the bathroom and walked to the sink. I steadied myself, placing both hands on the white basin, resting for a moment, before turning on the faucet and cupping my hands to collect water to rinse my mouth. When I was finished, I opened the door to find her motioning again. We picked up Tatiana along the way. Tatiana looked tired and anxious. I reached to touch her shoulder, but I pulled back my hand. *Are my growing feelings for her one-sided?* I hated the uncertainty and wanted to tell her how I felt, but I figured it was the last thing I should bring up.

We were back in the cafeteria line, and I casually placed my message on top of the napkins Tatiana had stacked on her tray. She, in turn, moved her flatware to prevent it from flying away. We made our way to a table, and, on cue, one of our "friends" strode across the room to join us. I noticed Tatiana had removed the napkin I'd placed on her tray.

While Tatiana and I were eating, I laid a napkin on top of my knife, and when I reached for my napkin again, I gripped the knife underneath and brought them both to my lap. I felt the knife slip off my lap and I grabbed for it, guessing where it was in mid-air. I couldn't do it again if I tried a hundred times, but, somehow, I pinched the tip of the blade between thumb and index finger before it hit the floor. My heart was pounding hard. I was able to get it back to my seat and eventually into my pocket. I looked at the guard sitting at our table and at the others sitting near to us, and none of them appeared interested in my movements.

I calmed down, we finished eating, and we were taken back to our rooms. When we arrived at Tatiana's door, I smiled and stood there for a moment, wanting to say something more before walking away, but our escort tugged at my shirt. I said a simple "Goodbye" and turned toward my room. My chaperone let me in, and I heard the lock engage after the door closed. I put my ear to the door and could hear him walking away.

I turned out the lights and pulled the knife from my pocket. Quietly, I slid the blade between the edge of the door and the metal plate. I was able to move the lock's bolt by leveraging the blade against it. I continued prying against the bolt, when, suddenly, it popped free, and the door swung open several inches. I reached for the knob, hoping to quickly pull it back to its closed position but instead missed, and the door opened further. I reached again and pulled the door closed. I listened for footsteps but heard nothing. *Damn it . . . another close call.* I turned on the light and grabbed a napkin.

I think we should try to leave tonight.
I am afraid we're out of time.
I'll be outside your door at 2 AM.
Be ready.

I slipped the napkin into my pocket and lay down on my bed.

As the hours went by, I became more nervous thinking about the escape. *So many things could go wrong, I thought. If we're caught, I don't know what they'll do. Even if we manage to get out of the building, how are we going make it home?* My worries made my head hurt. I closed my eyes and tried to relax. I slept, dreaming I was being pursued by a dark, nebulous figure. I awoke when Vera unlocked my door and told me it was time for dinner.

We walked the hall to Tatiana's room and found her ready. She smiled when she looked at me. *I would like to see her smile more often.* Joining the line, we picked up our trays, and I took the napkin from my pocket. I was about to set it on top of Tatiana's tray, as I'd done before, when a lady cleaning the counter bumped Tatiana, causing her tray to slide toward my hand, pinching my finger between her tray and mine. The napkin fell from my hand, and, as it did, it unfolded and landed like a pup tent on the tile floor. I leaned down to pick it up, but the cleaning lady picked it up for me. I reached out to take it, and she shook her head.

She said something in Russian, and Tatiana translated. "She said she will get you a clean one."

I shook my head nervously and said, "Five-second rule." holding out my hand.

Tatiana said something else in Russian, and the lady smiled politely, handing it back to me.

"What did you tell her?"

"I told her you were a stupid American trying to save the world's environment one napkin at a time," Tatiana said, as another small smile graced her face.

I put my head down to hide my grin—it was one of those "we-shouldn't-be-laughing" moments, but we couldn't help ourselves. When we were finished at the counter, I carefully placed the napkin on her tray. Before we reached our table, she had somehow slipped the napkin in her pocket. This time, our male companion was already seated. To be a smart-ass, I started walking to another table, but the man cleared his throat in an unequivocal command to sit. I smiled as I turned back, but he wasn't amused.

Tatiana didn't know it yet, but at two in the morning, I was going to break out of my room and come for her. I would ask her to try to find a ride while I was taking care of the rest of the master plan. Maybe she could find the keys to a maintenance van. Any set of wheels would work. My goal was to open the supply room and find the most flammable liquids I could. The next stop was the computer room. I hoped no one would be there.

We finished our dinner and were led to our rooms. When we reached her room, I looked into her eyes for some sense of reassurance, but, like before, the moment was quickly interrupted by our unfeeling caretaker. I looked over my shoulder as we started to my room and saw Tatiana still looking in my direction.

Once back in my cement box, I flopped down on the bed and set my watch's alarm, thinking about the night to come. It was good that I had slept earlier, because I was unable to now.

About 1:40 a.m., I got up to get ready, making sure to turn off my alarm. I layered up with some of the men's scrubs that were in my room, carried my backpack to the door, and set it on the floor. I put my ear to the door and listened. All was silent. As quietly as I could, I used the knife to coax the lock's bolt to move just far enough to allow the door to open. I stowed my knife, slung my backpack over my shoulder, and left. The hall that was normally as bright as day was now dimly lit. I moved quickly to Tatiana's door and pulled out the knife. Getting the bolt to move as I wanted was more difficult standing outside the door. It took four tries, but I was finally successful. I opened the door and found Tatiana ready.

"I want to ask you something before we do this. Should we use Antiquity and try to change what's happened instead of this semi-suicidal escape plan? I mean, Antiquity might be able to reverse almost everything that's happened without all the risk."

Tatiana looked at the floor and said nothing for a moment.

"I don't think so. They can always find me again, and I don't know what Antiquity would do to you."

I nodded in agreement.

"Okay, then. Let's do this," I asserted, trying to sound as positive as I could under the circumstances.

"I'm going to see if I can break into the supply room. If you're cool with it, you try to find some keys to a car, truck, motorcycle—anything's better than nothing," I said, rocking toe to heel with nervous energy.

"I'll try," Tatiana said anxiously.

"If something goes wrong, yell as loud as you can. Do you understand?"

"I understand."

I found the storage closet and began working the lock, when, suddenly, I heard the distant echo of hard-soled shoes. The sound was getting closer. I intensified my efforts as the footsteps grew closer. My knife slipped, and the bolt made a clicking sound that rang out. Whoever was walking stopped for a moment. The footsteps started my way again but at a brisker pace. I was ready to grab my things and run when my knife cooperated. I slipped into the closet just before the stranger entered the hall. I quietly closed the door, turning the knob to stop it from making a clicking noise.

My heart was pounding, and I was trying to control my breathing. I heard my unknown pursuer trying doors as he or she walked. We had been careful to close and latch each of our doors. The knob on my door suddenly moved, and the door rattled. I froze. Again the door shook hard, and I was afraid it wasn't securely latched. Just as I was preparing to tackle whoever stood outside if the door burst open, the knob was set free. I relaxed and listened as the sound of the shoe soles grew distant. I thought about Tatiana and hoped she wouldn't be discovered.

When I could no longer hear the echo of the stranger's shoes, I opened the door wide enough to faintly light the room. All the labels were Russian, so I had to go by sense of smell. I didn't recognize everything I took a whiff of, but I recognized several, and they were certainly flammable. Lacquer thinner and acetone were top of the list. Even the little I smelled gave me a rush, and I didn't want to stay in this closet for long. I jammed several cans into my backpack and set another two by the door. I opened the door wider and surveyed the hallway. It looked empty. I made sure to relock the door before heading toward the computer room with my incendiaries. As I walked forward, I kept listening but could hear nothing. I was now standing before the door to the computer room. I slowly opened the door and looked for people. I saw nothing but the glow from the many screens scattered throughout the room. I fully opened the door and made my entrance. I walked directly to the computer they had arranged for me, quickly took it apart, and removed my hard drive. I found Tatiana's machine and put it into my backpack after removing the cans.

Opening the first can, I paused. I knew what I had to do, but it was so wrong at the same time. I said a silent *I'm sorry* to the Man Upstairs and proceeded to move from area to area, being careful not to paint myself into a corner. When I was done pouring the last of it, I stepped back. Vapors were filling the room, and any spark would ignite the surroundings—and me along with it. I backed up to the exit with a flat panel that was tied to a long extension cord. I opened the door and set my pack in the hall. I held the door with my foot and raised the monitor above my head. I hurled it toward the center of the room. It skipped, and, as it broke apart, a small arc of electricity danced across the disintegrating screen like a sparkler. I dove for the wall.

The room exploded, blowing the doors open violently, with one coming completely off its hinges. My ears were ringing as I grabbed my gear and ran like a jaguar giving chase. I ripped round the corner, and, as I did, I saw a man holding Tatiana by the neck. I was moving too fast to put on the brakes and surprised them both as I slammed into them at full bore, knocking the pair to the cement floor. The man cracked his head forcefully against the wall. He didn't move. Tatiana looked at me like I was a madman— appropriate under the circumstances.

"Look in his pockets," Tatiana said, grabbing my arm.

We found a key set. I was getting ready to run when Tatiana stopped me.

"Come here," she said waving her hand. I followed her, running to a security room two doors down. She opened a drawer full of cell phones.

"Do you think we could get one of these to work for us?" she asked intently.

"Sweet! Good job, Tatiana," I said, reaching for my iPhone.

"That's your phone?"

"Yeah, they took it from me when I got here," I said, checking to see if it still had some battery life.

We ran toward the doors that led outside; we both slowed and looked at each other. Without saying a word, we ran back to the man lying in the hall, who still appeared dead. We each grabbed an arm and dragged him to the door. The building was ablaze. We burst into the icy air. We dragged him as far away from the blazing structure as we could and let go. Tatiana didn't lose a beat pressing the fob's button hoping to see the flash of taillights. An SUV a hundred feet away responded. We ran toward the truck, but, halfway there, I lost footing on the ice-covered lot and went down hard. The frozen gravel ripped through my jeans and opened a gash just above my left knee. I had to get to my feet and to the vehicle, but the throbbing pain prevented me from doing anything but hold my leg. Tatiana was back at my side.

"We've got to go, Jeffery! Hurry! I'll help you," she said frantically, as we heard the sound of distant sirens.

She got me to my feet and helped me slide my backpack over my shoulder. I limped toward the SUV. I could feel warm blood as it ran down my shin.

"You drive," I said, trying to catch my breath.

Tatiana muttered something in Russian.

"I don't drive."

"Crap! Give me the keys," I gasped. I used the body of the truck to brace myself and maneuvered over to the driver's side. I hopped in awkwardly, banging my knee against the car's frame.

"That helped," I said, wishing I could stop to rub the pain away.

I started the truck, shifted into drive, and mashed the pedal. We spun wildly on the snowy ground, and I struggled to gain control. I backed off the accelerator, and the truck responded as we found the road leading away from the property.

"Tell me where to go. I have no idea where we are," I said, starting to laugh from pure nerves. I looked at the screen that was illuminating the dash. "Is that GPS?" I pointed.

"Yes, yes, I think so," Tatiana said as she started pressing menu options. "Keep your eyes on the road!" she demanded.

"This road is coming to an end. We have to choose left or right. I can guess."

"Shush . . . I am almost finished," she insisted. Tatiana finished by pushing a button; the console started barking in Russian. "Go left, Jeffery," Tatiana snapped, her adrenaline still surging.

"Where are we going?"

"Back to my home. I know it's dangerous, but I have to see my mom," she said with desperation in her voice.

We could see the orange glow of fire against the clouds.

"That was Dmitri you knocked down. I asked him why he was with them. He said they offered him so much money that he couldn't walk away."

I glanced at her but didn't know what to say. We saw the flashing lights of the emergency vehicles ahead. They screamed by, sirens blaring. Snow flew in their wake.

A sudden burning pain reminded me of my leg.

"Can you reach my bag? I need something to wrap around my leg," I asked, reaching down to ascertain the damage.

"Yes."

She handed me a t-shirt, and I wadded it into a ball, using it to put pressure on the laceration, which was still oozing.

"What else can I do to help?"

"Nothing . . . thanks . . . I think it's okay."

We said very little for the next several miles as we pressed on into the darkness. We were both trying to fathom what might come next.

CHAPTER 33

THE SENATOR CALLED BACK and informed Jeffery's parents that Jeffery had flown to Russia. The airline confirmed Jeffery, or someone of Jeffery's description, was on the flight and had deplaned in Lensk. The senator struggled to manage his emotions when thinking about Jeffery's family, as he, too, had a son Jeffery's age. The senator had taken the step of acquiring the name of a man who could help Jeffery's father should he choose to follow Jeffery to Lensk.

Indeed, Jeffery's father was preparing for travel. There was no reasonable explanation why Jeffery had embarked on this bizarre excursion. Adding to the mystery of Jeffery's disappearance was the disappearance of his hard drive. Nothing made sense. Jeffery's father had minimal confidence he could accomplish anything once in Russia, but he felt compelled to try.

A ping abruptly filled the silence. It was Jeffery.

no battery i am okay no time to explain i will text again soon trust me

They looked at each other, hoping one or the other would have an epiphany, but none came. At least their son was alive. Jeffery's father called the senator to let him know. They weren't sure what to do but elected to wait for Jeffery to call or text again.

Yoko received a similar text from Jeffery with one addition—Dmitri was involved in Tatiana's kidnapping. Jeffery warned Yoko to be on alert.

Jeffery's parents were in the kitchen, warming up yesterday's soup, when they heard the doorbell ring.

"Were you expecting someone?"

"No . . . no one," she answered.

Jeffery's father wiped his hands and went to answer the door. He opened it to find three men in suits. Each of them displayed their IDs and asked if they could come in. After examining their credentials, Jeffery's father stepped back, indicating they should enter.

"Are you Jeffery McGregor's father? I believe your first name is Austin? And you must be Mrs. McGregor—Alice— am I correct?" the man in the gray suit stated in a business-like manner.

"Right on all counts," Austin replied. "Honey, these men are from the CIA."

Austin and Alice offered their guests a seat and sat opposite on their sofa.

"What's this all about?" Austin asked, looking at the man who seemed to be the spokesman.

"It's good you're seated, because what I am about to tell you is going to be difficult to believe," he said, hesitating before continuing. "We believe Jeffery has been engaged in playing a computer game, although 'game' isn't an appropriate description. It's called "Antiquity," and we believe it is capable of altering historical events."

"'Altering'? You mean the game simulates historical what-ifs?" Alice asked.

"That's a logical assumption, Mrs. McGregor," said one of the other men this time, "but by some unknown mechanism, the game more than simulates . . . it alters real-world outcomes."

"Are you hearing this?" Alice asked, turning to look at her husband, who was still trying to digest what had been said.

The man in gray continued.

"We recently detected activity, and, when Senator Johnson inquired about your son, we were confident we were correct. The only people who sense these historical changes are those who are currently playing or have played "Antiquity" in the past. We have several employees who were former players, and they're constantly watching. They can remember what the world was like before the changes occurred. Small changes are difficult to identify, but large historical alterations are clear to them," he said, pausing to allow the McGregors to catch up.

Austin and Alice sat staring, beginning to question who was really sitting in their living room.

"I'm afraid I still don't understand." Alice shook her head. "Are you claiming this, what did you call it—'Antiquity'?—can change history, and I wouldn't know it happened?" she finished.

"As insane as it sounds, that is exactly what I am saying. There are some who feel they can leverage Antiquity to advantage. We believe Jeffery was somehow coerced into traveling to Russia to work with one of these parties. Is Jeffery's computer here?" he asked with interest.

"His computer is, but the hard drive is gone."

"That's unfortunate, but not surprising. We think an organization associated with the Russian government is keenly aware of Antiquity's capabilities, and we're concerned that Jeffery—and perhaps other players Jeffery may know—have been targeted. We're attempting to locate Jeffery and find a way to get him back to the U.S., but it won't be easy. I wish we had more time to explain this extraordinary situation, but, for now, you will need to trust—as hard as that may be. Do you know if Jeffery has been communicating with new friends lately?" he asked in a serious tone.

"Not that I know of," Austin answered, looking to Alice.

"He didn't mention anyone to me," Alice said, searching her memory.

The room went silent, and the men stood, preparing to leave.

"What can we do?" Austin asked.

"If Jeffery calls or texts, find out anything you can about where he is. Other than that, you'd better leave things to us. Even with our resources, as I said, this will be a challenge."

Austin accompanied them to the door, shaking each of their hands, prolonging his handshake with the man in gray. "Please," Austin said as he looked intently at the man with whom he was shaking hands.

"I understand. We'll do all we know to do."

Jeffery's father closed the door, after which he slowly walked to the sofa. His wife hadn't moved a muscle.

CHAPTER 34

WE PUSHED THROUGH THE DARK RUSSIAN NIGHT. By the kilometer count on the display, we were nearing her home. Tatiana was asleep, and I smiled when I looked her way. I hated to roust her, but I wanted to make sure the Russian GPS was leading where she expected.

"Tatiana . . . Tatiana," I said softly. "Tatiana . . . are you awake?"

She opened her eyes and stretched.

She smiled and said, "Доброе утро."

"What?"

"Oh, 'Good morning.'"

"Are we going the right way? I don't trust the GPS, especially when I don't understand it. I've been following the arrows, but I want to make sure. I am pretty sleepy," I said with a nod.

"Yes . . . yes, we aren't far. When we arrive, I think we should park away from my home and walk. I don't want to be caught off guard again," she said with a shudder.

"I'm good with that. You okay?" I asked, returning a question.

"I never want to go through that again. They held me . . . they pushed that cloth in my face . . . ." She stopped and looked away.

I didn't know what to say, so I said nothing. I drove on in silence. After a few twists and turns, we arrived. She directed me down a road where I found a spot that would obscure the vehicle, at least in part.

My muscles were sore from last night and from sitting. I carefully stretched to loosen up. The cut above my knee had stopped bleeding, and I didn't want it starting again.

As Jeffery stretched, Tatiana watched. She liked his hair, a dusty brown that showed a hint of red in the sunlight. His eyes were green and clear. He was thin but fit, and his bright smile seemed to come from more than just the muscles in his face. It was genuine and somehow filled with optimism. Jeffery turned and noticed Tatiana's glance. "What? So don't laugh. I was tight," I said, not realizing I'd broken into the smile she'd just envisioned.

She smiled back. "Are you finished?" I gave her a thumbs-up, and we started walking.

"Don't speak if we meet anyone," Tatiana suggested.

"Just in case, should you and I have the same story for why I'm here?"

"I will say you are an exchange student, but I won't stop to answer questions," Tatiana said as we rounded a corner.

"Okay."

Tatiana slowed down and then stopped.

"My house is on the corner across the way—you see? It's the gray one," she pointed. "We will pass by the house next to mine, so we can walk to my house from the back."

"Do you see anything that looks jacked-up?" I asked as we picked up pace.

"'Jacked-up.' What is 'jacked-up'?"

"Sorry—do you see anything that doesn't look right?"

"Not so far," she said, a bit annoyed that I was distracting her.

We made our way down the snow-covered street, and I followed her closely as we cut through her neighbor's property. Tatiana crouched down as we entered the area behind her house. There were two windows and one door on the rear of the small, yet sturdy-looking, building. It was clad in weathered wood, which took on a herringbone pattern at points. The trim around the windows was ornate, like something on a gingerbread house.

"That is the kitchen window; that door opens to the kitchen, and the other is my bedroom window," she said as she changed her posture to get even lower.

We crept to a spot just below the kitchen window. The windows weren't far above the ground. We knelt for a moment, both of us getting ready in case we had to react quickly. "Let me look first. I don't want to scare mom to death," she whispered as she put her hand on the sill and slowly pulled herself high enough to see. At first she saw nothing, but, after a few moments, she saw her mom walk into the kitchen.

"Mom looks tired," Tatiana said in a concerned voice. "Let's look in my window." She continued moving swiftly to the next window. "Make sure no one comes behind us, Jeffery," Tatiana said as she positioned her body in preparation for peering into her window.

"Do you see anything that looks, well, 'jacked-up'?"

Tatiana rolled her eyes and smiled.

"No, Jeffery. Nothing looks 'jacked-up,'" she said, moving toward the rear door. She reached for the doorknob. "Locked."

She knelt and lifted a pot that still held a remnant of last year's greenery and found a key.

"You hide keys in Russia, too."

"Certainly," she said, putting the key in the lock. "Jeffery, do you see that stick of wood against the house?" she directed.

"The axe handle?"

"Yes, get it.

"I'll go in first. You stay back. I'll scream if I see Dmitri or one of his thugs. You get behind them, and hit them with the handle," she said, looking to see if I understood. I nodded, not sure if I liked the plan, but I didn't have any better ideas.

Tatiana slowly turned the knob. The door made a *swooshing* sound as it cleared the frame. She entered, and I kept out of view. I was tense, and my back was pressed against the cold outside wall. I heard a scream come from the kitchen. I wasted no time in busting through the door, axe-handle ready to hit something as hard as I could.

"Mom!" Tatiana screeched in return. "Is anyone here?" Tatiana asked in Russian, putting her finger to her lips. Her mom answered, and Tatiana translated her answer.

"She said my sister is in her room, listening to her loud music on headphones."

"Mom, get her, and come right back," she barked, changing channels to Russian.

"Jeffery, I think we should gather some things and leave now. They can't be far behind, and they're going to want to kill someone. I'm afraid it will be mom or my sister."

"I'll bring the car around."

"Good . . . take the road that runs past the next row of houses," she said, taking my hand in hers and dragging me to the window to show me. "I will get my family ready to leave."

I ran, all the while looking from side to side nervously. I got the SUV running and found the road Tatiana had instructed me to take. Pulling to the curb, I stopped fifty feet from Tatiana's back door. Her mother was crying, and they were closing their cases when I entered the house. Tatiana said something in Russian, and we started for the car. We loaded their few possessions, and I turned the truck around so that we could leave by the same back road. Stopping at a side street about three football fields away from her house, we saw two black SUVs come to a rapid stop across from Tatiana's home.

"God, Jeffery—back up! Don't let them see us," she said intensely. Her mother wailed something indiscernible that made me jump, and I accidentally revved the engine.

"Mom," her sister scolded.

Mumbling and angry at myself for not keeping my cool, I backed into a nearby drive and managed to get the vehicle pointed in another direction.

"We'll go a different way. Turn left at the next street," she motioned.

My eyes darted between road and rearview mirror, expecting to see them closing behind.

"We'll need to get gas before long," I said, turning briefly to look at Tatiana. She had been talking to her mother and sister almost nonstop since we'd left their home.

"There's a town a few kilometers ahead; we can stop there. We have some money," Tatiana declared and then switched back to Russian.

"I have American dollars. We can cash them in for Russian money," I said, wanting to contribute.

They were in pure Russian mode. I don't know if they heard me. I went back to being chauffeur.

We stopped to fuel up and were back on the road. My passengers had talked themselves all out. It was strange, after all the talking, to hear nothing. So I filled the void.

"Do you have a destination in mind?"

"We are going to a small ski resort I visited long ago. My mom knows the people—it's all we know to do. Are you tired?" she asked thoughtfully.

"I am tired, but I'm okay. I'll sleep better tonight. Is the resort far?"

"Two hours. I can drive, but you won't like it."

"Okay, keep me awake and headed in the right direction," I said, keeping both hands on the wheel.

The plan to keep me awake was less than perfect, given that my copilot was running on fumes. My head was bobbing, and I came to twice to find our SUV in the wrong lane. I nudged Tatiana when we rolled past a sign with a skier in silhouette, and, after fifteen minutes of "Turn-here, turn-there," we pulled into the picturesque resort.

We were greeted with smiles, embraces, and cheek kisses. Our hosts assisted in unloading our few bags, and I was instructed to pull the SUV into a maintenance shed a few hundred feet from where we stood. My muscles were tired, and I fell twice in heavy snow on my way back up the hill. There were half-a-dozen houses scattered about that looked like they belonged on a Swiss mountainside. The owners put us up in a unit with a tiny loft reached by climbing a narrow wooden staircase that skirted the wall in the main room. It was furnished with a cot and would be mine. The women would share a queen-sized bed which filled most of the only true bedroom. Tight quarters they were, but we felt lucky to have them.

We were getting settled when we heard a knock. What little adrenaline my system was able to generate did little to prepare me for a brawl, but I tried to convince myself I could handle what came through the door. Tatiana's sister asked who it was, and the wife of the owner answered. When the door was opened, we could see her and her husband carrying trays loaded with covered dishes. We sincerely thanked them before saying "Goodnight." They smiled and chattered as they trod the snowy path leading away from our temporary refuge.

The room filled with aromas of chicken, potatoes, roasted vegetables, warm homemade rolls, and streusel with small scoops of vanilla ice cream already melting from the warmth of the pastry. It was hard to imagine a meal of greater appeal, and I could see that each of us, worn down from fatigue and stress, was humbled by the generosity bestowed on us. The little ski house that was to be our home for the night seemed a paradise. Tatiana's mom said a blessing, of which I understood little, but the meaning wasn't lost on me—a blessing was certainly in order. We finished our feast, and, between the warmth of the room and our full stomachs, we were not long for the world.

"The owner said they have Wi-Fi in the clubhouse. I know you want to contact your family. Goodnight, Jeffery," she muttered, struggling to keep her eyes open.

"Goodnight, Tatiana."

I climbed the miniature staircase to my cot, plugged in my phone, and knew no more for the night.

CHAPTER 35

ANOTHER DAY ELAPSED, and there was no further word from Jeffery. Jeffery's father was holding the business card left by the gray-suited CIA agent. Ironically his name was Jeffery—Jeffery Thompson.

"I think I should call the CIA to see if they've learned anything. I feel completely useless," Austin mumbled. As he reached for the landline, a ping announced a text.

"It's Jeffery! Look," Alice said as she entered her password, revealing the full message.

too long a story we were being held we escaped but they are after us i am okay love you i will text when I can

"I don't believe what was said about Antiquity. I don't know what to make of what was said, but it might help Jeffery if we let him know he doesn't have to keep Antiquity a secret," Alice said.

Jeffery's father nodded in agreement.

We know about Antiquity. CIA says Russian government knows, too. Maybe they are chasing you. CIA may give you help. Tell us where you are.

She showed her text to Austin and sent the message. Under normal circumstances, a brief moment would pass with little thought, but, now, time stretched like strands of taffy—finally another ping.

you know??? antiquity can change history tell cia there are four of us IT IS FOUR OR NOTHING!! we are at small resort called something like snow dove maybe 110 miles north west of lensk text when you know something

After receiving Jeffery's return text, they called agent Thompson.

"Give me the name of the resort again. You said 110 miles NW of Lensk? And there are four who need safe passage? The detail is important. Let me ask, did the word 'Antiquity' get sent as text?" There was silence while the agent waited for an answer.

"Yes, we wanted Jeffery to know. The name 'Antiquity' was used twice, once by us and once by Jeffery. We wanted Jeffery to feel confident, so we said that the CIA had visited us." Austin's forehead wrinkled with concern.

"I'm sure their surveillance teams are keying on the word 'Antiquity.' They probably assume we're involved. At this point it's spilt milk, and we have to act. We may be able to throw them off the hunt, at least for a short time. Stay by the phone." The agent was gone, with no "Goodbye."

Alice firmly grasped Austin's arm without saying a word.

CHAPTER 36

STILL ALIVE I WAS KIDNAPPED jeffery came to help me they want us to use turns for them dmitri betrayed me be careful don't worry about us they may come after you

Yoko knew Tatiana was sincere when she said, "Don't worry," though worry was a way of life for Yoko. Her concern was not only for her new friends but also for her parents. The entire insane escapade had become more than she could hold inside. Yoko didn't know how to tell her parents, but she knew the danger was real, and she had to tell them one way or another.

Yoko's parents were preparing dinner when she stepped into the kitchen.

"I need to tell you something. It's important. Can you please sit with me?

"This will sound crazy, and I won't be able to prove anything. You must trust that I am telling the truth and haven't lost my mind."

Yoko's parents turned to each other and said more with a look than written or spoken words could convey. They placed their kitchen knives on the counter and put their arms around Yoko as they walked to their family room.

Yoko started at the beginning and didn't stop talking until she had exhausted all. Everything was now on the table.

At first, Yoko's parents said nothing. To say it was a lot to absorb was an understatement.

"Are you sure these people you're communicating with are good and telling you the truth?" her father asked, with great sensitivity.

"Yes, father—this isn't my teenage imagination. Antiquity is real. I don't know how it's able to do what it does, but it's real. We are truly in danger. I wish I could somehow show you, but I can't."

"And you say the game will not work if we are watching?" he asked, wanting to believe.

"No, father. The game will work, but you won't be able to tell that it worked because you won't remember. It's complicated."

"I don't understand this. It is beyond what is reasonable to believe," he said, stopping her.

After a long awkward silence, he continued.

"Yoko, if you say this is true, then I stand with you," he said as he reached for her.

Yoko fought the tears beginning to well in her eyes. Her father and mother held her until they saw a hint of a smile light her face.

How they would keep safe was next on the agenda. They had no plan, yet Yoko felt safer knowing her family was with her.

CHAPTER 37

AGENT THOMPSON ARRANGED for several additional texts and phone calls to be made designed to replicate Jeffery's phone from multiple locations outside Lensk, thinking a little diversion might buy time. Though the odds of successfully extracting them from Russia under these circumstances were long, the CIA was doing what they did best. Travel arrangements for four were quickly planned, dispatching several CIA resources within driving distance of the resort. The question of who would reach Jeffery and his companions first—friend or foe—would be answered shortly.

The phone rang, and Austin answered with trepidation, afraid he would receive terrible news about Jeffery.

"Is this Mr. McGregor?"

"Yes. Who is this?" Austin retorted.

"This is agent Thompson. Do not text Jeffery. We are in a race, and we don't want to give the bad guys any advantage. Should Jeffery text you, you need to call me before you respond. Do you understand?" he finished curtly.

"Yes . . . yes, I understand."

"Good. I know this is difficult. Be assured, we are doing everything we can. I'll update you as soon as there is something to report."

The call went dead.

"Who was that?" Alice asked as she walked in from the kitchen, drying her hands.

"It was agent Thompson. He instructed us not to text Jeffery because it might give Jeffery's pursuers an advantage. We need to inform him of any texts Jeffery sends," Austin said, looking at the phone.

Alice's face reflected the weight of worry. She nodded and turned to go back into the kitchen.

CHAPTER 38

TATIANA AND I WERE SITTING AT A TABLE in the resort's lodge. The smoke-steeped, cedar-clad walls gave off a rich aroma. I was wishing we were there to ski and hang out instead of hiding. Tatiana seemed at peace for the first time since I'd met her. I hated to interrupt her moment of quietude with reality.

"Tatiana, we need to get out of Russia. You know these guys aren't going to stop. When we went back to get your mom and sister, we escaped recapture by the skin of our ass."

"Must you speak that way?"

"What?" I asked, trying to understand her disapproving tone.

"This is my home, my family's home. Are you saying we should have left my mom and my sister behind? You can go on without us, but I won't abandon them," she snapped in frustration.

"Tatiana, I'm not saying that. There's no way I would leave your family behind. I came here to do whatever I need to do to help. I'm saying that you and your family aren't safe here—at least not right now. Those men aren't going to stop, and I don't know how to live on the run."

"We could give them what they want. Maybe then they'll leave us alone. I'm tired and scared, and I want things to be like they were. I want to go back to school and be with my friends," she said, her voice trailing away.

I didn't have the heart to remind her that we both knew what they'd do if they had their way, and we'd already agreed using Antiquity to undo things wasn't the solution. I said nothing more.

She stared at the fire but wasn't focused on it. Her gaze was more distant, more detached, like she was looking at the far horizon.

She lowered her head for a moment before turning to speak. "Where would we go?" she said, barely audibly.

"The only place I know anything about is the U.S. I'm not saying we should go there, but I think we could get help if that's our choice."

Tatiana looked at me and then looked away. My heart told me to move to her side of the table and hold her, but I stayed where I was. I still didn't know how she felt, and I suck at reading signals.

"I guess we don't have a choice," she said, adding nothing more.

After sitting without saying a word for what seemed like forever, I told her we'd better eat something and get ready to go.

Tatiana shut down her laptop, and we ordered food to take back to the room.

We ate Russian sandwiches; when we were finished, we packed up our few things.

"Do you think I should text my mom?" I asked, looking at my phone.

"I wouldn't. I'm sure they're monitoring everything we do."

"Right," I said, slipping my phone into my bag.

I carefully moved the drapes away from the window to form a small gap so I could see the entrance to the resort. I didn't see anything to raise a red flag. As I was ready to close the drape, a movement caught my eye. It was almost imperceptible.

I sharpened my gaze . . . one, two, and three. Three figures camouflaged in white were making their way over the crest that led to the resort.

"Tatiana." I said urgently.

Tatiana came to the window.

"You see what I see?"

"My God—how did they find us?" Tatiana asked, not expecting an answer. She quickly switched to Russian.

Alena announced something, and her mom repeated it. Now they were moving like they were on fire.

"Tatiana," I said, pointing to the small door at the back of the cabin.

She turned to look and nodded. Alena was helping her mom with her coat. We grabbed our bags and left. I set off in a different direction, hoping to confuse our pursuers. I'd like to say we ran, but the knee-deep snow made walking nearly impossible. I looped back around and found Tatiana's mom on her knees. Tatiana said her mom had fallen three times. There was nothing to do but hide. Crawling under the boughs of a massive evergreen, we all knew we didn't have a chance. Those giving chase would hardly need to be expert trackers. Underneath it was dark and still, and I could almost stand at the tree's center. Little in the way of light filtered through the densely covered branches. Under other circumstances, it would have been peaceful, but, for us, it was a place of last resort. We had no gun, no knife—no weapon of any kind to make a stand. We were at the mercy of the white-suited figures we had seen through the window. We sat quietly, waiting, naively hoping this storm would pass.

Before long, we heard footsteps. We couldn't see our hunters through the dense, snow-covered foliage, but they were there just the same.

"Jeffery McGregor? Jeffery?" a man's voice rang out.

I looked at Tatiana and kept silent.

"My name is Jim, and I'm CIA. Unless you want to join the Romanovs as a long-term resident, we have to go now."

We struggled to leave our enclave, but, in short order, we were back in the depth of the snow, looking at three men.

"Are you able to travel?" Jim asked—he appeared to be the lead.

"Yes, but Tatiana's mother will need help," I answered.

"Good. Let's move," he said.

We were walking back toward the chalet when the rattle of gunfire broke the snowy stillness.

"Down," Jim yelled in an intense, gravelly voice as he searched for cover.

I wanted to do something to find more protection, but any move would expose us even more.

"Shit!" one of the CIA guys cussed. "They winged me."

Jim barked back a question, "How bad?"

"I'll make it," he shouted as the firing continued. "I nailed the bastard," the same voice retorted.

The mini-war raged on.

"Got another one," the third CIA man grunted.

The firing continued, and our side was winning. Finally Jim stood and said what we wanted to hear: "I think the last one's down."

The other two slowly made their way up the hill to assess the state of the enemy.

They returned and gave Jim a simple nod, saying our assailants were no longer a threat.

"Okay, we have to get this show on the road. Aaron—you said you were hit?" Jim asked.

"I took one in my off hand, but it was clean. In and out," he responded, removing his glove and grimacing. "It stings but not badly, all things considered," he finished as the third of the trio was pulling out a first-aid kit.

I was just starting to let down my shoulders when Alena let out a dreadful scream.

"Mom! Mom! Help her! Please! Mom!" she wailed in desperate, halting sobs.

Tatiana was on her knees, pulling her mother to her. Blood was everywhere.

"Mama! Please, mama! Hold on!" Tatiana begged. "Jeffery, do something! Save her!" she cried.

I will never forget how real the pain was and how little I could do to help. A surge of memories passed through my head—my sister's face as she was dying was front and center. For a moment, I couldn't move.

The deep-red color of their mother's blood stood in sharp contrast against the pure-white, newly fallen snow. Jim and the other two ran to her side and knelt. Jim felt for a pulse under her neck. Tatiana and Alena couldn't talk, still on their knees, holding her. Tears streamed down their cheeks.

"I'm sorry, but she's gone—and I hate to be the one to say this, but we have to keep moving. More militias will be sent to stop us. They're probably on the way. There's nothing more that can be done for her," he said pulling at Alena. I put my arms under Tatiana's and tried to raise her. It felt like gravity was ten times stronger within that small patch of blood-drenched ground.

"Tatiana, if we can get somewhere safe, we can try using Antiquity," I said. "But if we're dead, we can't help anyone. We'd better listen to him," I said, finally helping her to her feet.

Alena was standing, but nothing could stop her relentless weeping as we walked away from their mother, lying motionless.

"Don't look back," I said as we followed our rescuers.

We ran and walked until we made it to two SUVs. I pulled a t-shirt from my backpack and wet it thoroughly with a bottle of water I found on the rear floor of the SUV. I helped Tatiana and Alena clean their hands and arms.

"You have my name," Jim said. "The guy with the hole in his hand is Aaron, and that's Eric."

"You know me. I'm Jeffery, and this is Alena and Tatiana," I said, feeling like I should say something else, but nothing that my brain generated seemed appropriate.

While Jim and the other two were pulling off their white suits, Tatiana removed her laptop from her backpack and held it firmly. Alena, Tatiana, and I got into the same truck with Jim and Aaron. We hit the road.

"Do you have a way to connect to the internet?" Tatiana asked as soon as we slid into our seats.

"You can't send anything that will give away our position," he said, making sure we understood.

"I won't," Tatiana said as he handed Tatiana a MiFi stick, which she quickly plugged into her USB port. She booted up her machine and looked at her battery—good charge.

"The stick you gave me is asking for a password," Tatiana said anxiously.

"Hand your machine up here," the man said.

Jim leaned to Aaron and whispered the code.

"You should be good now," Aaron said, handing the computer back to Tatiana. Tatiana took it from him with two hands, making sure she had a firm hold. She launched Antiquity and waited for the game to load. Every second seemed like an hour. She grabbed my leg and turned the screen so I could see it.

Reverse the event of Tatiana and Alena's mother's death.

Tatiana looked at me. I nodded.

She pressed "Send."

Your event is being administered. You will be notified when complete.

Alena was pale. She stared blankly at the landscape as we rolled on. An hour or so went by, and the driver asked if we were done with his MiFi hot spot.

"Almost," I said as I nudged Tatiana to check Antiquity. *Your event change is complete.*

We looked at each other, expecting to vanish or vaporize any second. We weren't sure what was going to happen. I handed the stick back to Jim and thanked him. Tatiana turned off her computer and closed the top.

I looked at Alena and saw she had fallen asleep, her head leaning against the window. I sank down in my seat and let my head find a comfortable position. Before long, I felt the weight of Tatiana's head fall against my chest.

It was cold, but peaceful, under the great evergreen's branches. My thoughts were muddled. This scene was so familiar. I looked to Tatiana, and the expression on her face probably resembled mine.

"Have we been here before?" I whispered.

"I don't think so," she whispered, questioning her memory.

"Jeffery McGregor? Jeffery?" a man's voice resounded.

"My name is Jim, and I'm CIA. Unless you want to join the Romanovs as a long-term resident, we have to go now."

We struggled to leave our shady enclave, but we managed and were back in the depth of the snow, looking at three men.

"Tatiana, Antiquity. Your mom—do you remember? This is happening again," I said, grabbing her arm.

"What?"

"When you saved me after Sage blew me up, I was like you. I didn't remember until it was almost too late. I think because I've been through this before, I'm recognizing it faster. Don't you remember that your mom was shot?"

Her eyes widened, "The blood . . . I remember blood."

"Jeffery . . . *now!*" his voice now stern.

"We have to go. Tell your mom to stay low to the ground. Antiquity changed the outcome, but we're not going to take chances."

"Back that way . . . snipers," I said, pointing.

"Did you see them?" Jim asked.

"Sort of," I answered, not wanting to explain.

"Everyone, let's hustle!" he said, trying to get us to safety.

The echo of gunfire filled the air.

"Shit! Everyone down," Jim said, waving his hand.

We were, once again, face down in the snow. It burned against my face, but that was the least of my worries. Finally, like before, our side silenced those firing at us.

"Move," Jim again barked an order.

I turned to look at Tatiana's mother.

"No!" I shouted.

Alena started screaming—just as she had the first time we went through this nightmare.

"Mama!" Alena screamed again.

Blood was staining the soft, white landscape.

"Mom!" Tatiana now joined the chorus of screams. I landed on my knees beside them, trying to make sense of this. Alena and Tatiana were holding their mother and crying uncontrollably. Nothing had changed—*what the hell?*

I got control of my head and looked at their mom carefully. Something was different. Their mom was sitting up. She was crying but fully conscious.

"Alena, Tatiana, let me see her," I said, sliding closer. "It's her arm."

The bullet had ripped through her clothing, and blood was flowing from the bullet's exit point, but the bullet hadn't ripped off the top of her head, as in version one's insanity.

"Move back!" Jim said as he knelt. He got her sleeve up enough to inspect the wound, which was still bleeding. It wasn't pretty. Compared to the exit point, the wound where the bullet had entered was dainty. The flesh where the bullet left her arm was torn apart, opening a view to her muscle and tissue only a surgeon would be comfortable with. It wasn't a vision I wanted to remember.

"Good. It somehow missed the major vessels," he said.

He pulled a kit from his backpack, selected a plastic pouch, and ripped off the top of the bag. He poured powder all over the torn flesh.

"What's the powder going to do?" Tatiana asked as the tension began to subside.

"It causes the blood to coagulate rapidly," Jim answered as he pulled a roll of gauze from his pack.

Within minutes, he had dressed the wound. He helped their mom get to her feet.

"For the last time—let's get the hell out of Dodge," Jim yelled.

As we walked, Jim introduced Aaron and Eric. This time, Aaron hadn't been shot. I decided I would stop trying to understand how Antiquity worked.

We struggled through the snow as we helped Mrs. Smirnov. She was hurting but alive. Antiquity had saved her life, but I hoped I would never have to live through this again. It took longer than version one to get to the SUVs, but we were traveling in relative safety. Aaron pulled a syringe from a black case and pulled off the needle's cap with his teeth.

"What is it?" Tatiana asked with trepidation.

"Tetanus, antibiotic, and something to take the edge off," he said, moving quickly to find a spot of exposed flesh on Mrs. Smirnov's arm.

Almost immediately her muscles relaxed from the rigor-mortis-like state of a few moments ago.

Tatiana leaned to me and asked, "'Take the edge off'?"

"He gave your mom something to take the pain away."

I looked at Alena, and, when she looked back at me, she smiled ever so slightly. Tatiana and I were the only ones riding down the road who knew of a different history.

"Thank God she's alive," Tatiana whispered.

"Thank God," I repeated, leaning back against the seat.

CHAPTER 39

THE QUASI-GOVERNMENT GROUP to which Dmitri now belonged had not been deterred by the destruction Jeffery had caused. Not only had they dispatched several teams to hunt down Tatiana and Jeffery, but they had moved to an auxiliary computer center to carry on the work that was interrupted.

Dmitri and two other previous Antiquity players were attempting to determine where the last two players resided. They had been overconfident in their ability to control Jeffery and Tatiana, and had missed an opportunity to examine email communication between the pair. It was a critical mistake, and Dmitri was under extreme pressure to bring the other players into the fold.

They knew two things about Guru: her estranged boyfriend was named "Ren," and she had used Antiquity to eliminate her mother's cancer. Japan was obvious. Antiquity would have already altered Yoko's Facebook postings and medical records to reflect her mom's present state, but Dmitri knew Antiquity left crumbs that could be followed. He was betting he could find Facebook pages that weren't private and contained critical information.

Dmitri was using software developed to scour public Facebook pages, looking for key words and phrases. "Ren." by itself, would cast too wide a net, because the name was common in Japan, but when coupled with "illness" and "mother," the number of pages in play was reduced significantly. After reading through the remaining translated pages, Dmitri found one in which he had a high degree of confidence: a girl named Yoko Yamagata who lived in Nagano City. The page included a description of a mother who was battling a recent case of pneumonia which occurred at a time coincident with the request Yoko had made of Antiquity. Dimitri knew, for reasons not understood, Antiquity would frequently lessen the original conditions but not eliminate problems entirely. In addition, there were no more references to Ren after a date which matched Antiquity notices regarding her breakup with Ren. *One down*, Dmitri thought.

Sage was a bigger problem. He had ensured a plane would explode, and he'd caused the destruction of the International Space Station, which, had it not been reversed, would have cost lives and led to the brink of war. The software used to find a Facebook link yielded no useful information. The explosion at Jeffery's home had been reversed, but Antiquity wasn't involved in causing the explosion. Perhaps Sage had had a hand in it. This would take more time.

Dmitri decided to act in Yoko's case while the effort to determine who Sage was continued. Besides, if they were successful in abducting Yoko, her email could provide vital clues. He picked up his cell phone and made a single call.

After explaining his research, Dimitri heard the words he needed to hear: "I want her."

"I will take care of it," Dmitri replied in the same tongue, and the call went dead.

Dmitri called a second number and set the wheels in motion. Yoko and her family were now being hunted.

CHAPTER 40

TATIANA WOKE TO THE SOUND of the men's voices. Their tone was intense. Aaron was looking backward.

"A vehicle is closing fast. It might be nothing, but I wouldn't bet your Rolex on it."

"Yeah, my Rolex—bite me," Jim smirked, shaking his head.

"We need to be ready," Aaron said as he picked up the radio, signaling Eric in the SUV riding ahead. Eric slowed to let us pass. Aaron began preparing for battle. He loaded a pistol and handed it to Jim. He also loaded two others and set aside several clips.

"The pack with the red patch—hand it to me," Aaron ordered.

Tatiana reached back and pulled the heavy pack from behind the seat.

"Hurry," Aaron said.

She struggled to get the pack within Aaron's range, who grabbed it as if it were full of air. She soon saw what was in the pack, as he extracted four or five cylindrical objects.

"Hopefully we won't need these puppies, but, like the scoutmaster says, 'Be prepared,'" Aaron said with a sense of pride.

"Are those grenades?" Tatiana asked with uneasy curiosity, eyeing the explosives that were just inches away.

"They ain't party favors," Aaron said as he continued to perform his tasks.

The approaching truck was now clearly visible and continued to close the gap. Jeffery looked at the speedometer: 85 kilometers an hour on snow-covered roads. The hour or so of peace they'd experienced was a memory. The sound of shots fired dimly resonated.

"It's them, alright. They're shooting at Eric's tires," Aaron said sternly. "Let's see if we can even things out a bit," he continued.

"Get as low as you can," Jim shouted back at us.

Alena helped her mom move as low as she could before she covered her mom with her body. Tatiana and I slid as close to the floor as we could, turning into amateur contortionists. Aaron had the largest of the pistols in his hand. They radioed Eric to shift as far left as he could on the count of three. Aaron dropped the power window. Frigid air streamed into the interior of our truck. Eric must have been following the plan, because Aaron began shooting. The concussion of the shots was deafening. A sharp cracking sound suddenly echoed from the side window.

"Careful. Those strays can cause problems," Jim said in monotone, recognizing that a shot from our pursuers had caromed off our side window. The bullet left a long, white line but didn't break the glass. Aaron was hanging out the window. He fired three more rounds.

"I think I nailed their block! I see smoke, and they're dropping back," he said as he pulled himself back inside and raised the window.

Eric radioed, "Nice shooting, but I'm losing tire pressure. They must have hit pay dirt."

"Tell him I'll stop in two kilometers. I want to crest that hill to get out of range," Jim barked. "He'll have to ride with us. We have no time to fix a blown tire," Jim instructed tersely. We pulled over, and Jim said one of us would need to move to the back seat.

"I can," Tatiana and I said in unison.

"All the better. Both of you move to the back," he ordered.

It wasn't premeditated, but sharing the back seat with Tatiana was fine with me. Within minutes, we were racing down the road again.

"This won't be the end of it. I'm sure they were being cautious because of our passengers, but they will take bigger chances next time. If they can't get their hands on these kids, they won't want anyone else to," Jim said as he turned and looked behind at us.

"What's the plan?" I asked, wanting to know if we had a chance of surviving.

"There's an airstrip about fifty miles from here. If we stay on schedule, the plan is to rendezvous with a plane and a flight out of Russia," Jim said, keeping his eyes steady on the road ahead.

I looked at Tatiana. Jim kept his foot to the floor. I felt the SUV slide on more than one occasion, and I tightened up each time, expecting to end upside down in a snowdrift, but Jim somehow kept it on the road. The sun was getting closer to the horizon, and I worried the plane wouldn't be able to land for lack of light. After another forty minutes of travel, we rounded a large curve, at which point Jim pulled off and started across a snow-covered field, throwing us in all directions in the process. He finally slowed as he crowned a knoll. A hundred yards ahead, there was a strip that looked like it had been plowed to an icy sheen. To me, it looked more like a small skating rink than an airstrip. He drove to the edge of our so-called "runway" and stopped. All the guys jumped out and opened the tailgate.

"Jeffery," Jim grunted brusquely.

"Yeah."

"Can you can step away from your girlfriend for a minute and give us a hand?" he asked as he was opening another bag. I felt my face turning red, like a teenage Rudolph, except that it wasn't only my nose; my whole face glowed. A small smile graced Tatiana's face. As I got out, the cold air and darkening afternoon light made me feel like we would never get out of Russia alive. I fought my growing sense of doom and walked to the rear of the vehicle, still feeling the heat from my flushed face. Jim handed me a small nylon bag.

"Inside that bag are LEDs," he said, pulling back the zipper, revealing spherical plastic objects.

He turned one over, revealing a switch. He slid the switch, and the pod began to glow bright amber.

"We need to frame this runway every twenty paces or so—move quickly. Our schedule is tight. We'll each start at a corner and work back to the midpoint."

We did as he said, and, by the time I dropped my final pod at the runway's center, my hands were numb from the cold. When framed by the glow of the lights, it took on the look of a real runway. We walked back to the SUV and climbed in to get warm.

"Will you be coming with us?" I questioned.

"No, we leave by roadway," Jim said curtly.

We sat in silence, listening. Before long, we heard the low drone of engines. The sound grew in intensity, but we still couldn't see the craft.

"He'll be flying dark," Aaron said. "There—I see him now," Aaron said, opening his door.

"Let's get ready. That means you, too," Jim said looking back at us.

We climbed out and grabbed our bags and backpacks. The CIA boys pulled on vests, and each slung an assault rifle over his shoulder. The shadowy outline of the plane approached and dropped further in preparation for landing. It looked more like a helicopter than winged craft, seeming to hover before touching down and rolling to a stop close to the end of the temporary strip.

"That was awesome," I said under my breath.

My dad was a small-plane pilot, and he'd taken me flying many times. I learned the basics, but I couldn't imagine making that landing. The pilot turned her around in preparation to take off. The plane's door opened, and a small staircase folded down. The pilot looked in our direction and saluted. The guys trotted over and shook hands. Our CIA chaperones looked like they could run ten miles and not break a sweat, each of them stout athletes who looked as if they'd come from the same mold.

We slowly followed, helping Mrs. Smirnov across the snow-covered field.

"No copilot?" Jim asked.

"No, this was a last-minute deal, and we weren't sure we could take on the extra weight. It'll be alright," the pilot winked.

They instructed us to board. Mrs. Smirnov was having a tough time getting up the stairs, and we helped her on first. I made sure Alena, Tatiana, and Mrs. Smirnov were seated before walking back to the door.

"Thanks for saving our butts."

"Anytime," Jim said with a smile.

The pilot was climbing the stairs when I heard a shot. The pilot recoiled and cussed. Another shot, this time the bullet ricocheted off the stair rail, almost hitting the pilot a second time. The CIA guys were each down on one knee and returning fire.

"Get the hell out of here," Jim yelled.

The pilot had been shot in his shoulder, and the red circle forming on his shirt was expanding. I stepped partway down the steps and helped the pilot on.

"Pull that big lever," he said, wincing. I did as he asked; the stairway collapsed into a cavity, and the door swung shut. "The latch . . . lock it down," he said, rocking backward as he put his hand over his wounded shoulder. I struggled for a moment before it engaged.

"Follow me," he said as he labored to walk to the cockpit.

I helped him into his seat. Outside we heard a barrage of gunfire.

"Sit in the copilot's seat," he said using his head as a pointer. "There, the throttle. Push it toward the front at a steady pace . . . now!" he said loudly.

I did as he asked. The plane's engines roared, and we started moving down the runway.

"All the way now," he insisted.

The plane banged and rattled as it lurched forward. The end of our makeshift runway was approaching quickly.

"This is going to be close," he said, pulling back on the yoke with his one good arm. "You! Help me pull back on the damn yoke—hard!" he shouted.

I grabbed the yoke in front of me and pulled hard, like he said. The plane bounced a few times before it grudgingly left the frozen ground.

"Do you know how to fly?" he asked as his eyes closed and opened again.

"Not really."

"Not really . . . what the hell does that mean?" he asked bluntly.

"I mean, my dad taught me a few things, but I'm no pilot."

"That's better than nothin'. You see what's ahead? We need to weasel our way between those two mountains and then fly South-Southeast," he said now speaking with big sighs between words.

"South-Southeast. Yeah, okay," I mumbled back.

The mountains were getting closer, and things weren't looking good. I remember dad saying not to make it harder than it is, but I don't think dad ever pictured a scenario like this. I followed the pilot's lead, helping him to make the plane move as expected. We made it through the gap and eased into the South-Southeast course he had specified.

"Behind your seat . . . there's a cabinet door. Open it, and pull out the first-aid kit. I'm bleeding like a stuck hog," he said, looking at his shoulder.

The large Red Cross on the lid of the kit made for an easy find. "I'm getting lightheaded, and unless you're a pilot, I suggest you haul ass, or you'll be flying solo," the pilot said sarcastically.

"Get the damn scissors and cut away my shirt. There should also be a bag of powder—maybe Celox. Bring it to me, and hurry," he said, coughing.

I got to his side and nervously cut the material away. I got down to his skin, and, for the second time in a day, I was looking at a hole in a human body.

"Pour the powder before I bleed to death," he said as his eyes began to glaze over.

"Is he alright?" I heard a voice say behind me.

"I don't know. He's lost a lot of blood. His shirt is totally soaked."

Tatiana looked at the pilot's shoulder.

"Oh, God," she said uneasily.

I cut open the bag and dumped powder on the face of the wound. I leaned him forward, cut more fabric away, and dumped powder on the exit point, which looked much worse. The pilot was now dropping in and out of consciousness.

"Tatiana, please put bandages on him. I've got to do something to keep us flying. Say a prayer I'll be able to keep us in the air until he takes over again."

The sun was almost gone.

"You must do this, Jeffery," she said, more a command than a request.

I hardly heard what she said as I focused on trying to remember what dad taught me.

I kept whispering, "Don't make this harder than it is. Don't make this harder than it is."

Even in the dimming light, we could see mountains, maybe large hills, looming.

"You need to make the plane go up," she said.

I didn't respond and instead began pulling back on the yoke. The plane started rising, but suddenly lost power. We were dropping. *What the?* I remember dad warning me of this. What did he say? We were stalling! I needed to dive and start again, but the mountains were closer now. Downward we went, so I could gain control. When I pushed the plane to climb again, I gave it throttle. This time, the plane climbed smoothly.

"It's working, Jeffery," Tatiana said excitedly.

"I've got to keep focused."

"What can I do?" Tatiana asked sincerely.

"Keep praying. How's he doing?"

"His eyes are closed. I think he's asleep."

The sky was purple-blue. The last light was slipping over the western horizon.

"I don't know what to do. I can't see anymore," I said, trying to disguise the panic starting to creep into my gut.

Tatiana and I looked at each other. Our chance of living through this was next to nothing.

"The switch . . . under the flat panel . . . switch it on," the pilot said, coming back from the dead.

I did what he asked. The panel came to life. The image looked like a computer game I used to play. It was showing terrain.

"Is that radar?" I asked.

"Yes, son, that's radar. We have to get a grip on things, or we're going to go splat into one of these hills," he said, staring at it intensely.

He squinted at the panel. His eyes suddenly opened as if a grizzly were charging straight at us.

"Damn it, son! Pull her up!" he shouted.

I looked at the screen. It didn't take a genius to see that we were flying straight toward a large mass—a mountain.

"We're not going to make it!" He was pulling back on the yoke with his one good arm. I was doing the same and giving it every bit of gas it could swallow.

"Bank left! Bank left!" he yelled.

I pushed the floor pedal down with my foot and pulled back the yoke. She started turning hard. I swear I heard some branches nick the wing.

"Damn it, boy. That was close. Now level off," he groaned while holding his shoulder.

My heart was still beating like it was coming out of my chest, but the pilot had already calmed down, as if clipping a tree were something that happened every day.

Tatiana said something in Russian which needed no translation.

"We almost got intimate with the side of a hill," the pilot joked between coughs.

Tatiana looked at me, and I nodded in agreement. The look in her eyes was self-explanatory. She ducked and went back to her family.

"You need to teach me how to read that, in case you pass out again," I said, pointing at the panel.

He began talking, struggling with every word. When he finished a few minutes later, he said I was certified. He was running out of steam, hurting, and about to pass out again.

I kept my eyes glued to that little screen, and I maneuvered the best I could by what it said.

Tatiana came back. "How are you doing?"

"I'm okay. Sorry I was so intense earlier. I'm pretty freaked out about flying without the pilot helping me. The pilot said we need to keep all the lights off or we'll stick out like a sore thumb," I said, still focusing on the flat panel.

"'Sore thumb'?"

"An old saying . . . if your thumb was all swelled up, it sticks out . . . anyway," I said, looking at the pilot, who was out.

I continued to watch the screen and veered right or left or rose higher or lower. The pilot had said we needed to keep as low as possible. I stayed the South-Southeastern course as asked, but I knew more accurate directions would be needed soon. I didn't know if we were still in Russian airspace. According to the pilot's estimate, we should have been close to the border. Where were we to go after that? My brain was jumping from one thought to the next.

The radio screeched loudly and then clattered with a Russian-sounding voice.

"Tatiana!" I shouted.

"What's happened?" she asked, startled, as she re-entered the cabin.

"Sorry for yelling. I need to know what the man on the radio is saying."

The radio barked again. It was the same voice, but more insistent. Tatiana listened intently until the radio was quiet.

"He said we have to follow him to a landing area, or he will shoot us down," she said, looking at me with a "What now?" expression.

"Where are we?" the pilot asked, coughing and sounding even worse than before.

"I don't know, but we are being ordered to follow . . . ." I didn't finish because I was interrupted by a fighter jet that roared past.

"What are we being ordered to do?" the pilot asked, trying to think coherently.

"They said we have to follow them and then land," Tatiana answered. "They're military," she said.

The pilot looked at our coordinates.

"We're no longer in Russian airspace. They may still shoot us down, but we are over Kazakhstan," the pilot said, pointing to the radio.

He asked me to tune to a specific frequency. I handed him the mic, and he started speaking some sort of code. He repeated it several times before finally getting an acknowledgment.

Now we had a jet on each side. The pilot finished his message and directed me to tune to the original frequency.

He spoke in what sounded like Chinese.

"Maybe that will throw them for a minute," the pilot said with a pained smile.

The fighter pilot blared back, this time in broken English. I think he was trying to find a common language. Again, he commanded that we follow them to a landing zone.

"Come on," the pilot said, looking at what was left of his blood-covered shirt.

A different voice came over the radio, and, again, it sounded like Russian. I looked at Tatiana.

"They are saying the Russians are in violation of Kazakhstani airspace," she said anxiously.

Russian chatter bounced off the cabin walls.

"They're arguing. The Kazakhstani are demanding they leave immediately. The Russian is swearing," Tatiana said, briefly covering her ears.

The Russian planes suddenly broke away, screaming away just past our nose.

"That was dicey," the pilot proclaimed. "Follow the Kazakhstani jets," the pilot said, closing his eyes, leaning his head against his headrest.

"He has a lot of faith in me—more than I have."

"How difficult can it be?" Tatiana giggled.

"Go check on your mom," I said, shaking my head.

We continued to fly for another hour. I felt like I'd been standing on broken glass and trying not to move. My muscles ached. I wanted to be back on the ground.

The radio again came to life.

"Tatiana!" I called. "I need my translator."

Tatiana peeked into the cockpit.

"I thought you wanted me to leave," she said with a smirk.

"Only for a minute," I smiled.

The Russian from the radio was ringing in my ears.

"Can you make out what they're saying?"

"They say we need to prepare to land . . . we are maybe thirty minutes away."

"See if you can wake him up," I said, hoping the adventure was at an end.

Tatiana gently shook the pilot. His head rocked to the side, and his arm fell. Tatiana made a small, almost-imperceptible sound.

"Jeffery, I think he is dead. His hand is cold."

"Check his pulse!"

"He has no pulse," she said, lowering his arm.

I put my head down. "Shit . . . now I have to land a plane I can barely fly."

"What do we do?" Tatiana asked as she crouched by my side.

"I guess I'm going to land this bloody plane. You better tell our escorts to be ready for a rough landing."

Tatiana took the mic and communicated our problem. I could hear the dread in their response.

"They are asking if you have ever landed a plane."

"My dad let me try to land his plane once . . . it wasn't pretty. He had to bail me out, or we'd have been in the weeds."

"'Not pretty'? 'In the weeds'? How should I tell them what you mean?"

"Tell them I tried once, but it didn't go well," I said, straight-faced.

Tatiana translated what I said. The radio went quiet. After a few seconds, the radio crackled back to life.

"They said trying once is better than never," she translated, still listening. "They say they want you to follow the lead plane . . . he says he will guide you to the exact point . . . to let the plane touch the ground . . . he is going to describe the controls . . . you will need to . . . work with," Tatiana faithfully translated in spurts.

She continued translating, helping to locate everything they asked us to find. She said the pilot would guide us through each step.

"Tatiana, trade places with me. Hold this, and keep it in the same place."

She looked pale, but she didn't flinch. I got my arms under the pilot's, and I dragged him from his seat. I felt like I was doing something wrong, dragging him down the aisle-way, but I finally got him to the back. I looked at Alena and Mrs. Smirnov. Their faces couldn't hide their fear. They looked like I felt. I made sure they had their seat belts buckled. I tried to instill in them some sense of security by giving my best "I know what I'm doing" smile, but their expressions remained the same.

"Jeffery! They say it is time to start," Tatiana said, intensely.

I jumped in the pilot's seat, still coated in his blood. There was no time to clean it and no time to get grossed out. I could see the lights of the fighter ahead. He was dropping in altitude quickly. I wasn't tracking his flight path, and I knew when the radio squawked that I was being reprimanded.

"He says you need to stay with him, or we won't make the runway," Tatiana said nervously.

I let the plane drop quickly, too quickly. I dropped well below the altitude of the plane ahead. I leveled off and waited until he was at my height. It wasn't long before he was below me again. I followed, this time trying to control my descent more carefully. Better, I fell slightly below his position, but I was close. The ground was approaching, and my hands were sweating so much that it was difficult to keep a firm grip on the yoke. I wiped each hand on my pants, but it did little good. Tatiana continued to translate his commands, landing gear, flaps, prepare to begin braking; it was hard to stay with it as the ground neared. Tatiana translated his last two statements. When the pilot pulled up sharply, I was to let the plane drop to the ground. Suddenly the plane in front made an extreme climb. I did as he said, and the plane slammed hard onto the frozen runway, and then bounced, with another slam.

"The brakes, Tatiana! They said adjust the props," I yelled as I struggled to keep the plane centered. We were sliding and still moving much faster than we should be. We continued surging forward. The end of the runway was now in sight. I kept thinking, *God, please stop this plane.* The seat belts cut into me as the plane was finally showing signs of halting. I couldn't tell if it was fields or water past the end of our icy strip.

"Hold on!" I shouted as the front landing gear dug into the soft snow past the runway.

The rear of the plane rose up steeply as the plane slid violently sideways before it thumped back down hard—finally stopping. My head collided with the side window, and, for a moment, my vision was nothing but white sparkles. I rubbed my eyes, and my sight stabilized. I looked at Tatiana, and she looked at me. I put my head down against the sweaty yoke. Neither of us said anything. I cut back on the throttle, and the low drone of the idling engines was the only thing filling the void of our silence.

"If it's okay with you, I say we never try that again . . . way too fucking crazy."

We both laughed the kind of laugh that isn't appropriate for the circumstances—a laugh verging on hysteria, but it felt good. After a few minutes, I pulled myself together and unbuckled. I helped Tatiana to her feet, and we left the cockpit still half laughing.

The dead man stretched out on the floor cured us of our hysteria.

Alena and Mrs. Smirnov were dazed. Mrs. Smirnov was holding her wounded arm, but she was in one piece.

A pounding on the door startled all, and, friendly or not, I knew we didn't have a choice. I released the latch, the door opened, and the stairway unfolded. Several men in military attire stood in the drifting snow looking up at us. They weren't smiling, but they weren't shooting, either.

"Jeffery?" a man asked in a heavy accent.

"Yes," I answered as Tatiana slid to my side.

"Good, we have been, how do you say . . . ," he broke back into Russian.

"Expecting you," Tatiana said completing his sentence.

The man laughed and spoke a little while longer to Tatiana.

"He is saying we are safe and that an American Air Force plane is only an hour from landing. He said he will take us to get food and to a place where we can wait."

We helped the others out of the plane and explained what had happened to the pilot. I learned the soldier's name was Alibek. Alibek said he was sorry, and, further, that God must like us to have survived the landing. He was also kind enough to see to the pilot.

Alibek drove us to the mess hall, where we ate and warmed ourselves. We were exhausted and spoke little as we sat waiting. When Alibek re-entered the room, he was accompanied by a man in an American Air Force uniform.

He walked straight for us, took off his cap, and extended his hand first to my female companions and then to me.

"I am Captain Phillip Williams. I hear Alibek is treating you well. I also understand it was a harrowing journey. A bit of a miracle, I would say, and I'm very sorry to hear about your pilot."

He had a way about him that put you at ease.

"My instructions are to get you to America," he said looking at all of us. "I imagine this is very difficult for you," speaking directly to Tatiana and her family.

"Yes, very difficult," Tatiana and Alena answered in stereo.

I looked at Alena with surprise.

"This is the first I've heard you speak English, Alena," I smiled.

"I can't speak as well as Tatiana, but I understand what you say," Alena smiled subtly in return.

The captain turned to Alibek and asked how long it would be until the plane was refueled and ready to go. "Twenty minutes" was his answer. The captain saluted and smiled. Alibek walked away, and the captain instructed us to ready ourselves for a long flight. He said we would fuel again in Greece and then cross the Atlantic.

"I want to tell my parents I'm okay," I said, looking at the captain.

"Can you wait until we're airborne? Then I'll connect you through a secure channel," he asked rhetorically.

"Okay, but I really need to talk to them."

"I understand. If it makes you feel any better, a message was relayed back home to your folks when we got word you had landed—if you want to call it a landing," he said with a chuckle.

I laughed and thanked him for getting in touch with mom and dad.

"If you'll excuse me, I need to get a few things ready." He smiled once more and turned to leave.

I sat back down next to Tatiana and waited.

CHAPTER 41

THE MORNING AFTER YOKO'S HEARTFELT UNVEILING, she sat with her parents, and they talked about changes they could make to keep safe . . . simple, common-sense stuff. The doors were to be locked at all times. Before opening the door blindly, as they were used to, they would determine who was standing on the opposite side first. They would run errands together. They would begin using their home alarm system (it had been installed by the previous owner but had never been used). They would make sure Yoko always had a ride to and from school. All of these steps were departures from the easy, trusting way they had known.

Yoko knew her parents were denying all their instincts to believe her tale, and she appreciated what they had agreed upon, but she quietly feared it would not be enough.

The next few days were steady and normal. Yoko started to relax, feeling she'd exaggerated the danger confronting them.

Thursday began as the last few days had. She sat eating breakfast with her mom and dad—a new tradition. As trouble can sometimes do, it brought them closer. After cleaning up the morning's meal, Yoko and her father left the house. The first stop was Yoko's school; then her dad was off to his office. Yoko and her father laughed and talked as they pulled away from their home. Neither of them noticed two white work vans parked a block away.

One of the two vans pulled to the front of Yoko's home. The second followed Yoko and her father as they traveled the streets of the picturesque Japanese city. Yoko's mother would be taken first, considered the easiest, still recovering from pneumonia. The second target would be Mr. Yamagata. With both of her parents in jeopardy, Yoko would be more compliant.

Yoko's mother neglected to set the alarm. Three days had elapsed since the family had started their new safety measures, and Yoko's mother had yet to establish new habits. She loved classical music, and, like a teenager listening to the latest pop, she played it at high volume. Her mind was intently occupied with organizing the home office, and she didn't hear the door's lock being manipulated, nor did she hear the footsteps of the men behind her as they approached. She was subdued before she uttered a sound.

Yoko's father was next. He was more difficult to apprehend. As he walked from his office to the tea room across the street, Yoko's father saw a man who needed help collecting papers that had fallen from his briefcase. He knelt, and, while reaching for a sheet being rustled by the breeze, he felt a sharp prick. He had wrestled as a student and gave the pair "helping" him to the back of the van all they could handle before the drug took effect. The man with the briefcase joined the others, and they drove away, leaving no trace of their deed. If a public camera, now so common everywhere, had captured images of what had occurred, it would look as though the two Russian men were helping Yoko's father to the van.

When Yoko's father didn't arrive at her school on time that afternoon, she thought that, perhaps a late meeting, which sometimes happened, had kept him. Her mind didn't connect the sting she felt with the trio of men who had brushed against her as she stood waiting for her father. She rubbed her arm, wondering why it was burning. The men who'd walked by Yoko now turned and caught her before she fell to the ground. She was loaded into the waiting van and, like her mother, hadn't succeeded in venturing a scream. The van sped away with Yoko and her father lying on the steel floor like sacks of trash ready for a landfill.

CHaPTeR 42

PRIOR TO LEAVING KAZAKHSTAN, we asked the captain if he knew about Antiquity. He said he'd been briefed. We told him we could use a turn to save the pilot's life. His answer surprised us. He said, "First, any remaining turns are extremely important and need to be used only after weighing all the alternatives. Secondly, the pilot was dying of cancer. He didn't want anyone to know; he had made his peace with it. In fact, the pilot would have wanted it this way—going out in the service of his country instead of fading away in a hospital bed." We argued that we might be able to save him from the cancer, but the captain said we couldn't solve all the world's problems with Antiquity, arguing in return that life also needed to take its normal course.

It wasn't long before we were in the air again. I talked to my parents once we were airborne, and they were so overcome with emotion that even dad got choked up. They were looking forward to meeting my new Russian friends, and mom said she would tidy the spare bedrooms—it was mom's nature to help people. I apologized for all the trouble, but mom and dad wouldn't hear it. In their eyes, I was growing up, thinking more of others than myself. It felt good to hear them say so. They also told me that, no matter how crazy the situation, I needed to talk about it. So I asked them: if I had come to you and told you about a crazy history-changing computer game I could never prove really worked, and I needed to fly to Russia to save my friend, would that have been okay? After I put it that way, they laughed and agreed that this was an extraordinary case.

I was in and out of sleep and an intense series of dreams. In one, I landed a plane on its roof while the pilot who died cussed and slapped my back. He yelled, "Well done, kid," and everyone applauded. In a second, a bloodstain in the snow grew to an enormous size. I tried to run, but, in the dream, my feet were bare and frozen to the ground, and the blood rose to my knees. The last was pleasant; I told Tatiana how I felt about her. I kissed her, and she smiled and asked me to hold her. Waking was painful, but I wasn't given a choice.

I turned and looked at Tatiana. She looked pale and troubled.

"What's wrong?"

"I had this dream," she said, looking at me intently.

"I had some messed-up dreams too."

"You don't understand. I dreamed that Yoko is in trouble—both her and her family. It was real, Jeffery. I know it was. I must send her an email."

Tatiana was on a mission and left my side before we could talk further.

"Captain, I need the internet. It is very important. Is there a way to connect while flying?"

He hesitated. "As long as you are not sending emails or messages with the word 'Antiquity,' I think we can take a chance.

"There's a CAT5 cable coiled up about shoulder high. Plug and play," he said, pointing toward the cable.

Tatiana fired up her laptop and tested the connection with a Google search—all good. Launching Antiquity, she could see she hadn't received any email from Yoko. Tatiana wrote to Yoko to ask if everything was well. She hoped for an immediate reply. Five minutes, ten minutes, twenty minutes . . . nothing.

"Captain, what time is it in Japan?" Tatiana asked.

The captain looked at his watch and paused.

"I would put it about 6:00 p.m. or so. Why Japan?" he asked in return.

"I have a friend who lives there."

"Jeffery, did Yoko say what school she goes to?" Tatiana asked, her concern growing.

"She said she was in high school, but I don't think she said which school."

I changed seats to see if Tatiana needed any help. Tatiana found the email Yoko had sent in which she gave her full name and the name of her home city.

"What can I do?" I asked, trying to help.

"I need to find her school," Tatiana answered, impatiently.

"Did you try her Facebook page?"

"No, I didn't. Good," she said.

Tatiana found Yoko's page and searched. She found a photo of Yoko standing with two friends in front of her school. Most of the school's name was displayed: Nagano Nishi High School. Tatiana Googled the phone number.

"Captain, so sorry to trouble you further, but I need to make a phone call."

"All right. Come up here, and I'll get you connected," he answered with a sigh.

It took a few seconds before the call connected and started to ring.

"Do you speak English?" Tatiana asked in her Russian accent when the phone was answered.

"Little," the voice responded.

"I need to speak to Yoko Yamagata. It is a family emergency," Tatiana stated firmly.

"Emergency, for Yoko Yamagata," the person repeated.

"Yes—emergency," Tatiana confirmed.

"Minute please," Tatiana heard as she tapped her fingers on the panel next to the phone.

"Excuse, sorry, Yoko not school today," the voice said.

"Are you sure?" Tatiana pressed.

"Yes, sure, Yoko not school today. Thank you," the phone went dead.

"She wasn't at school today. I know something is wrong," Tatiana said, looking at me as she walked back from the phone.

"I'm starting to believe you. See if you can find a home phone number for Yoko."

Tatiana started a new search. It took forever—one dead end after another, until she finally found a good site.

"There are three," she said.

"Call them all," I said as we both stood.

"We have to make a few more calls, sir," I said as we approached the captain.

"What's up, guys?" he asked before allowing us to make our calls.

"We have to tell him, Tatiana. We don't have a choice," I said, hoping she would agree.

"Tell me what?" the captain asked bluntly.

"We think our friend is in trouble. She's also an Antiquity player. The same people who kidnapped Tatiana may be after her."

"What leads you to believe she's in trouble?"

"We said we would write emails every day so that we would know everything was good. She hasn't written. We called her school, and she isn't there. We found three phone numbers in the town where she lives, and we want to call," Tatiana said without taking a breath.

The captain thought for a few minutes.

"Make your calls," the captain said, handing over the handset.

The first number rang. A woman answered.

"Yoko Yamagata," Tatiana said in her best Russian Japanese.

"No Yoko." The line went dead.

The second number rang. No answer.

The third number rang, and a man answered. Tatiana tried again: "Yoko Yamagata."

"Yoko, no, no, sorry, no Yoko here," the man said, apparently understanding Tatiana's version of Yoko's name.

We sat down and looked at the captain.

"What is the address of the house where there was no answer?" the captain asked.

The captain made a call of his own. We heard him say he wanted someone at the address in question double time.

About an hour later, a call came through. "No one home," the captain repeated. "The landlord let you in..and? A lamp was knocked over and a throw rug was all bunched up; other than that—nothing," the captain repeated as much for us as to clarify what he was hearing. "10–4," the captain stated, hanging up.

He sat thinking, before voicing a concern.

"I don't know if I believe what I've been told about Antiquity, but if I wanted to use it to my advantage, I would want as many turns . . . is that what they're called . . . as I could get my hands on. I would want you back. Could they force your friend to use a turn to get you back?"

Tatiana and I looked at each other.

"Oh, God," Tatiana said, taking a seat.

I started thinking about the scoreboard.

"Tatiana, if they make Yoko use a turn to reverse our escape, counting our turns together, they would come out at least four turns ahead. There's no way we could escape a second time."

The captain pulled his wallet out and took a card out of it. I didn't see the name, but I did see the acronym: CIA.

He picked up the phone, and, a few minutes later, he was explaining the scenario he expressed to us.

"I am being asked what the percent certainty is," he asked, expecting an immediate answer.

He covered the mouthpiece. "Given what I described, tell me how strongly you feel the chances are that I am correct," he said, softening his tone.

"100%," Tatiana answered determinedly.

"High nineties," I said. "I certainly don't want to be captive again."

"We are highly certain the scenario I described is accurate and imminent. Yes, sir," the captain said, hanging up the phone.

"You are to use Antiquity to beat them to the punch. Do whatever you can to reverse your friends' capture. I'm sure they have her parents as well. Our government will take steps to protect them if you are successful in liberating them," he said, stopping. Then he continued, "According to previous players helping our side, I won't remember this took place—*crazy!* What are you waiting for? Get busy."

Tatiana had Antiquity up on her screen. She typed the request and pressed "Send." I gave the captain a thumbs-up, and he returned one in kind.

We leaned back in our seats.

CHAPTER 43

YOKO WOKE. COLD AND LYING ON A MAT, her mouth was dry, and she found it difficult to swallow. Her mom and dad were already awake. She had a vague memory of being on an airplane, an uncomfortable memory of looking out a small window, a drugged sleep, and being sick with nausea.

"I am sure the effects of the anesthesia are still present," a man's voice suddenly echoed, bouncing from side to side in Yoko's head. "You will recover your faculties soon. When you are again lucid, we require your assistance. If you provide us with help, we will restore you to your lives. If you choose to resist, the lives you have known will be gone." The voice finished, still resonating in Yoko's brain.

The man left the room, and Yoko stood, dragging herself to a table. She sat and asked her mom and dad if they were alright. They nodded unconvincingly. Yoko let her head rest on the tabletop.

As time elapsed, their heads cleared. Yoko looked at their surroundings; they were stark. At one end was the table where they were sitting. At the other were three cots and a few gym mats. A small bathroom jutted off from the center of the room. There was nothing to aid an escape. Yoko stood and reached for the table to save from falling. She shuffled to the door and tried to turn the knob. It was locked. The door burst open, causing Yoko to stumble backward. An armed guard entered the room.

"You need something?" the guard asked in broken English. Yoko shook her head quickly in fear, and he left the room.

What had led to the fire and destruction at the IT site in Russia was simply a breakdown in security, and it would not be repeated.

Yoko walked to the bathroom and washed her face with cold water, trying to shake the remaining cobwebs.

"You should lie down," Yoko encouraged her mother.

Her mother elected to take Yoko's advice and made her way to a cot.

Her father had a concerned look on his face, but he looked more alert.

"I am afraid they are going to force you to do something that is not in your heart to do," he said, placing his hand on Yoko's.

Yoko knew what her father was saying. If she refused to comply, they could hurt her or her parents. Her stomach ached when she contemplated the scenario her father foresaw. If she could get word to her friends, maybe they could help, but she saw no way to accomplish this. All seemed impossible.

She looked at her father and turned to her mother, who was resting. She felt guilt and regret, and she blamed herself for their predicament. Yoko wished hers was the only life at risk.

Food was delivered, but there wasn't a good appetite in the room. Each of them forced the flavorless food into their bodies for nourishment's sake. When they finished, the guard made certain all the plastic utensils were accounted for. Surprisingly, he handed out toothbrushes, though he collected them once they'd been used. Their imprisoners were taking no chances.

Before the guard left the room, he instructed them to sleep, as they would be needed when morning came. Yoko did the only thing she knew to do before closing her eyes—she whispered a short prayer to whoever was listening in heaven.

The door opened loudly, and a man with a heavy Russian accent barked that it was time to get up. They weren't given much time to ready themselves. After finishing a small portion of watery porridge, they were taken to a room, where another man explained what Yoko was to provide.

"My name is Aleksei. Step one; you will reverse your friends' escape. We need their turns to accomplish our ends. Do you need any clarification?" the man asked rhetorically.

"I don't think Antiquity can undo something that complicated," Yoko answered in the dim chance her captors didn't understand Antiquity.

"Dmitri," Aleksei called into the adjacent room.

It was strange to see the man Tatiana had written about enter the room. He stood silent and looked cold and detached. When Tatiana described him in her email, he seemed mysterious and interesting. The man who stood before her now was zombie-like. Yoko could sense he was annoyed, wondering why he'd been summoned.

"Our guest has told me reversing the history of Tatiana and Jeffery's escape will be too difficult for Antiquity. What say you?" Aleksei asked, crossing his arms.

"She lies, is stupid, or is trying to buy time," Dmitri said coldly.

"You were her friend," Yoko said in condemnation.

"Friendship is overrated," Dmitri responded. "Are you finished with me?" Dmitri questioned impatiently.

"For now," Aleksei said and repeated, "for now."

Yoko studied Dmitri as he left the room and wondered what kind of bargain had been struck with Aleksei.

"You will comply with my request," Aleksei said, motioning for Yoko to rise.

"I won't help you," Yoko said with determination.

"You will," Aleksei said, his words cutting the air with promise.

Aleksei rattled a series of Russian words as he looked at the two guards standing one each by Yoko's parents. Without warning, the man who was standing beside Yoko's mother grabbed a handful of her hair and pulled her to her feet. Her mother screamed in pain and the sheer shock of such an unexpected act. Her father yelled and tried to rise in his wife's defense but was quickly overpowered and forced back to his seat.

The guard dragged Yoko's mother to the front of the room and forced her into a chair.

"Don't help them," Yoko's mother said defiantly.

"As brave as your mother pretends to be, I assure you her bravery will be short-lived," Aleksei said with a sense of pride. "Let's not make this difficult. If you do as we ask, this will all be over," he said, finishing with false sincerity.

"I can't help you. I can't betray my friends," Yoko said, following her mother's lead.

"Dmitri!" Aleksei again shouted.

"You're interrupting my work," Dmitri grumbled impatiently as he re-entered the room.

"I need two more guards. Bring them," Aleksei demanded in Russian.

Dmitri surveyed the room with indifference and left to do Aleksei's bidding. In eight minutes, Dmitri returned with two hulking Russians. Dmitri bowed in an act of defiance before leaving the room. Aleksei sternly commanded the new arrivals to position themselves beside Yoko and Yoko's mother, pointing to emphasize his wish. Aleksei continued blasting in Russian until the men at his service comprehended what he intended.

One man held Mrs. Yamagata, and the other held Yoko. Her father was already constrained by the guard who hadn't left his side. The second man, standing beside Yoko's mother, began bending one of her fingers backward, fighting the natural course human fingers were meant to follow. Yoko's mother began screaming with great intensity as the pain increased. The screams echoed in Yoko's head, leading to a queasiness that made her retch. Yoko struggled to free herself to go to her mother's aid, as did her father, but it was of no use. Her mother's finger made a hideous "Pop!" sound as it gave way to the pressure applied. Her finger now stood in a queer upright position. Yoko looked on helplessly watching as her mother's hand quivered. Aleksei and the others remained undaunted.

Her mother moaned and turned her head away to avoid looking at the damage that had been inflicted. Her father wept in a combination of anguish and anger.

"You see, Yoko? You will cooperate, or your family will suffer," Aleksei said, staring callously at Yoko.

"Don't do what he asks, Yoko," her mother said bravely, struggling to enunciate.

Aleksei roared at the guards to continue the torture. This time the guard grabbed two fingers and lifted them backwards from the surface of the table. Yoko's mother screamed in desperation.

"Stop . . . please . . . I will do what you want," Yoko said, breaking down.

Aleksei waved his hand, and the guards stopped.

"Don't you see? This pain could have been avoided. I take no pleasure in your suffering, but you must cooperate. Come with me into the next room so we can get started," Aleksei said in a sickeningly sweet voice.

"I won't move until you care for my mom," Yoko said, slamming her fist on the table.

"Very well; calm yourself," Aleksei said. "Take her to the infirmary, and bring some brandy to calm our nerves," he said, wiping his brow with a handkerchief.

Yoko and her father didn't budge until Yoko's mother returned to the room. Her hand was heavily bandaged, but she was calm.

"I gave her an injection to settle her down," a nurse said as she escorted Yoko's mother to a seat.

"The nurse is a fool. If Yoko becomes uncooperative, our interrogation will be less effective," Aleksei said in Russian.

Aleksei turned his attention back to Yoko, "It is time; no more delays. Bring her along," he ordered.

Yoko followed, a guard trailing close behind. She could see her computer at the table they were approaching. Antiquity's images filled the screen. It was waiting for her password. Dmitri occupied a chair in proximity to a vacant chair that was to be Yoko's. She slid into the chair and prepared to enter the password that, like each time before, had manifested clearly in her mind. She considered lying, telling them she could perceive no password, but she knew that would only bring more pain, and, eventually, they would get what they wanted. She keyed the letters, numbers, and various punctuation marks, and she was in.

"Good. Very good," Aleksei said, like a child who gets its way. "Do not waste time. Reverse your friends' escape," he blurted out.

Dmitri interrupted. "Give me a few moments. I'm confident I will be able to locate Sage if I analyze her email."

"Ten minutes—five would be more efficient," Aleksei emphasized.

Dmitri began digging through email, discovering that Jeffery's near-death experience had been due to a computer card sent by Sage. Knowing Jeffery's address and the approximate time of the board's delivery, Dmitri felt he had enough to pursue Sage.

"The computer is yours," Dmitri said, closing her email.

Dmitri stood and started walking away.

"Just a moment," Aleksei said, stopping Dmitri's progress. "I want you to review what she writes. There can be no more errors."

Dmitri stood beside Yoko and watched. As Yoko entered her first keystroke, Antiquity flashed a message, a message that was the result of Tatiana's event change initiated from a plane flying far above the earth's surface.

The kidnapping of player Guru and her family has been reversed by player Mystic.

No one initially spoke. It was as if the words weren't comprehensible, but as the meaning of the notice and its ramifications became clear, Aleksei went into a rage. His voice produced a growl, like an animal who had stepped on a great bear trap, feeling the teeth cut flesh and hit bone. His guttural sounds increased in volume and intensity, and he started smashing a set of nearby drinking glasses. Dmitri and Yoko closed their eyes as shards of glass flew in every direction.

"I WILL LOCK THEM AWAY! WE CAN REVERSE WHAT MYSTIC HAS DONE! I WILL KILL HER PARENTS!" Aleksei screamed, like a child throwing a tantrum. "It was you, Dmitri. Your insistence on reading the email," he raved on.

Dmitri knew that none of Aleksei's raving, no locked doors, not even death would stop Antiquity, but he knew they could fly to Japan and capture Yoko and her family once again. Aleksei would hear no logic, no matter how sound, until his anger subsided.

Yoko, her mom, and her dad started the morning sharing breakfast. Unlike Tatiana and Jeffery, who had experienced the strange sensation of reliving an event, Yoko didn't yet realize life was repeating. Living it was different than using a turn to change an event that affected people half a world away. A knock on the door made Yoko jump.

"Let me answer it," her father said as he stood and walked across the kitchen; he pulled a cleaver from the drawer.

Another knock. Yoko followed her father to the door.

"Who is it?" he asked sternly in his native Japanese.

"Do you speak English?" a voice asked, also in Japanese, from the door's far side.

"Yes," Yoko answered, stepping closer to the door.

"Can we come in and talk?" a man asked this time in English.

"Who are you? What do you want?" Yoko curtly asked.

"We represent the government of the United States. It is urgent we speak to you," the man responded.

Yoko looked at her father. Memories suddenly flooded Yoko's mind. Her recollection was so strong she felt unsteady and leaned against her father. "Dad, we were kidnapped. We were in Russia. My friends freed us using Antiquity," Yoko whispered.

Her father looked at her, trying to understand, but he was unable to comprehend. He allowed the blade to fall to the floor, and he put his arm round Yoko.

Yoko drew back to the moment and the people standing outside the door. *Maybe Tatiana and Jeffery arranged for this,*

Yoko thought, but she also remembered the torture her mother had endured, and she had no intention of opening the door until she was absolutely sure.

"Will you open the door slightly? You can get a look at my credentials," the man asked, explaining further the matter he had to discuss was urgent.

Yoko looked at her mother and father. She could tell they were uncertain as well.

"Keep the chain hooked," her father finally said.

Yoko unlocked the deadbolt but left the chain in place, as suggested. Yoko wearily looked through the small opening between the edge of the door and the doorjamb, observing the man who was ready to pass his ID through the crack between door and frame. Yoko grabbed it, quickly closed the door, and re-engaged the lock's bolt. Each of them examined the ID. It said he was an ambassador for the United States. Yoko used her phone and performed a search. She was surprised when his image and position came up. The picture was grainy and very dated, but everything seemed to be in place. After a moment's whispered discussion, they decided to trust those standing outside.

Yoko unlocked the door and removed the chain. She opened the door cautiously and allowed the men to enter. Yoko returned the ambassador's identification.

"Of course, you know my name is William. This is Payton and DeWayne."

The others nodded without speaking.

"We need to get you to a safe house. We were informed you were in danger of being abducted. There is little time to move on this. You need to prepare to leave immediately. Do you understand?" William asked.

Yoko acknowledged and let her mother and father know they'd better do as William suggested. Her parents were still confused over what was occurring.

They quickly packed. Yoko was careful to remember her PC.

"Ready?" William asked after everyone gathered in the living room. "Let's go, then," he said after receiving nods from Yoko and family.

As they started to move, Yoko noticed a tattoo on Payton's wrist as he reached to open the door. She knew that tattoo. Yoko felt her face flush. She had seen that tattoo on the guard holding her when her mother was being tortured. Yoko stopped.

"One moment, please. I want to bring another pair of shoes," Yoko said, trying to sound authentic.

She saw Payton glance at his tattoo, and he looked at William and Dewayne. Yoko was walking away when she felt the dart hit the back of her shoulder. The force of the impact shocked her, and her leg caught a table leg, sending a lamp crashing to the floor. Yoko's mother and father ran to help, but their would-be abductors moved quickly to subdue them, firing two more darts. Yoko's mind was dulling quickly. The nightmare was beginning anew.

Yoko felt herself being lifted. One of the men was supporting her, carrying her, making it look as if she were on her feet. Her parents were also being aided. As they cleared the doorway, Yoko heard a dull thud, and the man supporting her fell, resulting in a hard landing—her hip against the stoop. Yoko felt pain radiate from the point of contact but didn't have the wherewithal to rub it away. Even in her drugged state, she could tell a great scuffle was taking place. The body of another man fell beside her, his face staring straight into hers. He looked comedic, his expression strangely distorted. In a moment, all went quiet. Then she felt herself being lifted again. She hated the lack of control. A man was helping her down the stairs. Her parents were at the bottom of the staircase, being assisted by others. These weren't the men who a moment ago held them captive. The man helping her was wearing pleasant cologne and smelled clean. Her last moment of awareness was being helped into a vehicle before all went dark.

Yoko slowly came to and was in a hospital bed, groggy and hungover. An IV was irritating her arm. She reached to scratch but found her other arm strapped down. Opening her eyes wider, she could see hers wasn't the only bed in the room. She tried to make out who was sharing the space, but when she attempted to sharpen her focus, her head pounded, and she let her head fall back to the pillow. Beginning to nod off, she heard the rubbery-squeegee sound of shoes coming closer. Yoko opened her eyes and saw a nurse in scrubs standing by her bed. She struggled, thinking she was about to be sedated.

"How are you, sweetheart?" the woman asked in an accent rarely heard in Yoko's part of the world.

She was American. Yoko's father once entertained a couple from Alabama, and she never forgot their easy, gentle way of speaking.

Yoko was able to muster a small smile. "I don't know."

"Y'all have been through the wringer," the nurse said, watching Yoko fight to free her restrained arms. "We were worried you would come to and pull the IV. I know they'll bug you to death, honey. It's helping wash the drugs from your system," she said, ending with a comforting smile. "I'll loosen those straps."

"Where am I, and where are my parents?" Yoko asked, trying to swallow.

"You are in an American military hospital, and your parents are here, too. Rest, sweetheart—you need it," the nurse finished as she studied the monitor.

The nurse softly pulled Yoko's hair away from her face. The nurse's caring touch instantly calmed her down. Yoko closed her eyes and drifted into a deep sleep.

CHAPTER 44

ALENA WAS HAPPY that her mom was being cared for at the base's hospital wing and was saying so when Captain Williams came into the room, walking at a brisk pace.

"They damn near got 'em again," he enunciated twenty feet away from where Jeffery, Tatiana, and Alena were sitting. "I still have no memory of what happened before you used Antiquity, and I guess it doesn't matter. Our players, or *former* players, say they picked up on the change. I think the whole thing is nuts. Anyway, the Russians had some pretty authentic-looking IDs and must have convinced the Yamagatas. They drugged those poor souls and intended to haul them away when our boys interrupted their plans. It was close, but, thank God, we arrived in the nick of time. Yoko and her family are safe. I understand they're still sleeping it off, but you should be able to contact them before long. The Russians are having a conversation with our CIA friends. That's the rundown."

"When can we go back to my place?" Jeffery asked, his eyes fixed on Captain Williams' face.

"Not for a little while. I don't want you to feel like prisoners after everything you've been through, but we have some risk factors. One, we think the reach of this Russian organization is extensive. They have ties to the Russian mob, and they're no fun to deal with. We are assessing the situation as I speak. Two, Tatiana's mom is in no shape to travel and needs a few days to recover. Three, your parents are on their way. Four, you really need to talk to our people about Antiquity. Can you trust me just a little longer?" the captain finished, meeting my eyes.

I looked at Tatiana and Alena. Fatigue showed in their eyes.

"Can we eat something and rest?" Tatiana asked.

"Absolutely. Let me show you to your rooms, and then we'll get you something to eat. Normally, we don't allow this, but we are putting you up in the officers' quarters. You won't be far from each other, and the accommodations are a step up, maybe not five-star, but nice," Williams said, helping with their few bags.

After we were shown to our rooms, the captain introduced us to Lieutenant Jessica Cramer. She was all business but had heart. Jessica showed us to the officers' mess. The food was good, and we ate more than we should have. After that, we headed back to our rooms—mine was first. Tatiana stopped at my door. Alena kept walking. I don't know if Alena was picking up on something or if she just wanted to go to bed, but either way, it gave me a minute with Tatiana. Now, standing with her alone, I felt my face getting warm.

"Are you nervous?" Tatiana asked with a mischievous smile.

"'Nervous'? Why are you asking?" I babbled, glancing at the floor while running my hand through my hair.

"Because your face is all red."

"So, maybe a little."

"You were blown up by a bomb, you came to Russia to save me, you came up with a crazy escape plan, you flew a plane when the pilot died, and I make you nervous," Tatiana said, reaching down to clasp my hand.

"When you put it that way," I said with a laugh.

My eyes left my shoes and met hers. *Damn, they're beautiful!* She smiled warmly as she let go of my hand.

"Goodnight, Jeffery."

She walked away, and I didn't move off my mark. When she turned back to see if I was still there, I sent another smile across the gap between us.

Tatiana was in my head for some time before I extinguished my bedside light.

My night was fraught with another round of crazy dreams. This time I relived the explosion, except it wasn't at my house. I was badly burned and on the floor. I heard men's voices in the room next to me; they were laughing. No one came to help, and I realized I was in Sage's dwelling. Then another airplane dream. I was flying in dark skies and the only one on-board. The plane was running out of fuel and was over a large body of water. Panic was setting in, and I struggled to perform the simplest maneuvers. I awoke suddenly, covered in sweat. I fumbled in the dark until I found a dry t-shirt and tried to get a few minutes' more sleep. Rays of sun were beginning to clear the horizon. Lying in bed, I thought about how close to death we'd come. I sure as hell wasn't playing it safe.

Walking to the mess hall, I was flanked by men and women in uniform, all moving as if on a mission. I entered the hall and saw Tatiana sitting at a table with a tray of food. She had just started eating and waved to get my attention. Maybe it was stupid, but I gave her a mini-salute back. Like dad always said, "When in Rome . . . ."

I picked up my grub and walked to her table. Whether to sit next to her or across from her—that was the question. I decided to take the safer route and sit across from her. When she saw me heading for my "safe" seat, she stopped me.

"Sit here," she said, motioning to the seat beside her.

"Sure."

"I had terrible dreams. I got up to forget," she said, cutting her waffle into pie-shaped pieces.

"I visited the same dream world—nightmares all night. My mind doesn't know what's going on. When life is normal again, if it ever is, maybe my dreams will be less intense."

"I think my family and I won't be normal again," she said, stabbing at the lone piece of sausage on her plate.

"Starting a new life, I would be totally lost."

"I feel lost," she said quietly.

We sat through the rest of the meal without speaking. Even in silence, I felt comfortable sitting next to her.

I turned my head toward the door and saw Lieutenant Cramer walking toward us.

"Good morning," she said when she arrived at our table. "Captain Williams said he would like me to take you both to meet a few people."

"So, I'm waiting to meet my parents, and I know Tatiana wants to see her mom."

"I understand, but I'm afraid that, if we don't take advantage of this slice of time, there won't be another opportunity. Look, your parents won't be here for a few hours, and, Tatiana, as soon as you return, you can see your mother straight away. What do you say?"

I guess the Captain had sent her for a reason. She was persuasive.

I looked at Tatiana.

"Yes, okay," Tatiana answered.

I nodded, stood, and took back our trays.

"You'll need your coats," the lieutenant said when I returned.

We found a black SUV waiting and slid into the rear seat; our driver did the rest. From a distance, I could see the US Capitol building and the familiar DC landmarks. It wasn't long before we were pulling into CIA headquarters. Cramer walked us in. She handed an envelope to one of the men at the front security post and waited. After reading the contents, he picked up a phone and engaged in a short discussion. When he hung up, he folded the document, slipped it into the envelope, and handed it back to the lieutenant. A few minutes later, another woman in a business suit arrived.

"I will take it from here. My name is Catherine. Tatiana and Jeffery, I presume?" she said, though she knew who we were.

"Yes," I answered for us both.

The lieutenant extended her hand to us. "I will be heading back to base."

"You're not coming with us?" Tatiana questioned.

"No, my clearance doesn't reach this high, at least not yet," she said, smiling. "You're in good hands. I'll see you when you get back to base," she said, saluting and turning in sharp military fashion to leave.

We followed Catherine; her vibe was professional, yet distant. Given where she worked, her distance wasn't surprising. Loading into an elevator, my body was ready for a ride up, but the car headed downward, and it messed with my equilibrium. In short order, the doors opened to a brightly lit corridor. We followed without speaking—not even small talk—just the echo of her shoes as we walked down the tile floor. About halfway down the hallway, she slowed and lifted a card hanging from a lanyard round her neck. She waved it across a reader and opened the door. Inside the room, there were twenty or more people sitting at computers working so attentively that they hardly noticed our entrance. Catherine escorted us to an office located at the far end of the room. Again she swiped the card in front of reader and opened the door. Following her in, Catherine walked around her desk and took a seat.

"You're Antiquity players, if 'players' is the right word," she said with a sympathetic look. "It's okay. I know about Antiquity. I've never played, but I believe Antiquity is real. Previous players help us understand and analyze its activities. My superiors have a hard time with Antiquity because they can't remember what existed before, but for some reason, I'm able to remember small bits. I don't know how, but I do," she said, hoping she had gained our trust.

"I don't understand exactly why we're here. Captain Williams said you wanted to talk to us, but what do you want?"

"We want both of you to work with us. We know there are two other players, one being Yoko—I understand she's safe. I intend to talk to her about helping us—I'm hopeful. The last remaining player is Sage. We don't know who Sage is, but we assume he'll use his remaining turns to cause harm."

"'Work with you'?" Tatiana said, not sure she'd understood.

"Yes, I suppose that begs further explanation. We will help get you through school—high school and college. For this, you would consent to work for us, for a wage, to keep a watchful eye, and if necessary, use your remaining turns to help stabilize things," she said in a calm manner.

"'Stabilize things'?" I asked.

"Yes, I am not the first to lead this office. Several before me have worked to make certain those who use Antiquity to do harm were balanced by those who wish to accomplish good. It isn't an easy task, and there are judgment calls some would criticize, but we care and do all we know to do," Catherine said with sincerity.

"What is to stop the Russian men who captured me from coming after us?" Tatiana asked.

"We have concerns as well, but we have made inroads with Russian gangs and feel we have the resources to protect you and your families," she said, looking at both of us.

"Can we think about it? I want to talk to my parents," I said, looking at Tatiana and then back at Catherine.

"Absolutely. I want to talk to your parents as well. Please consider our offer carefully. This thing is bigger than you or me," she said as she stood and offered her hand.

She picked up the phone and simply said, "Ready."

We stepped out of her office, and she walked us to the door. There we were introduced to a man who escorted us back to the lobby, where we met the driver, who took us back to base.

CHAPTER 45

UNLIKE ALEKSEI, DMITRI DIDN'T INDULGE in regret. He found it a distraction and a waste of mental energy. Rather, Dmitri continued his efforts to locate Sage. What Dmitri wasn't able to discern through searches of public records, his programmers were able to find through less-mainstream approaches. Russia had a long history of cultivating exceptional hackers, and Dmitri's team boasted two of the best.

Dmitri's team had been successful in tracing the shipment of the sabotaged video card sent to Jeffery. They discovered that it had been shipped by a dead man. Dmitri expected the shipper of the card to be fictional. The fact that it was a real human, albeit a dead one, was effective if one wished to hide his or her activities. The transaction was made in cash—a further precaution taken by the shipper. The shipment had been made from a town located in the far southeast of Spain called Arocena. Obviously the individual shipping the card could have traveled to further obfuscate their activity, but it was a good starting point. Dmitri and his team estimated how much Sage had paid for such an effort and determined a sum of eight to twelve thousand dollars would have been required. Keeping that range in mind, his team looked through records at local banks to find withdrawals that qualified.

In the area of Arocena, two such withdrawals were uncovered. The first had been redeposited in a retirement account. The second, however, had no such trail. It was gone. The name on the account was Adolpho Delgado. Dmitri felt strongly this was Sage. Dmitri believed this lead was worth pursuing and arranged for a flight to Seville.

Dmitri landed on a Tuesday afternoon and rented a car for his drive to Arocena. His team prepared a detailed package outlining Adolpho's history, his current address, his mother's name, his absent father's name, his financial profile, and so on. Dmitri didn't know how Adolpho would react to Sage's veil being lifted. Arrangements were made for a weapon to be sent to his hotel in a series of packages that, in and of themselves, appeared innocuous, but when the components were assembled, they made up a pistol small enough to stow in a pocket.

Dmitri arrived in Arocena and decided to locate Adolpho's house to gain an understanding of points of entry and exit. After scouting the residence, he returned to his hotel and studied the information the team had amassed. Adolpho had a history. His school records indicated he'd struggled academically and behaviorally. His issues had begun when his father left the family, never to return. Adolpho was certainly not the first, or, sadly, the last child to face abandonment, but he never moved past it—at least that's what the paperwork implied. Now Adolpho was an angry man in his mid-thirties. Considering this, Dmitri felt it could be used to his advantage.

The following day was cloudy, with a freshening northeastern breeze. After having breakfast and tea, Dmitri drove to Adolpho's home. Dmitri could be charming when required, and as Adolpho's mother answered the door, he performed on schedule. Explaining that he and Adolpho were in school together for a short time, he said that he was back in town and thought it would be nice to pay him a visit.

"*¿Hablas ingles?*" Dmitri asked.

"No so good. Adolpho back in minute. He walk to buy paper. You wait?" she finished with a question.

"Yes, thank you."

"Tea?" Mrs. Delgado called from the kitchen.

"That would be splendid," Dmitri answered politely; his objective was to make her comfortable.

Within ten minutes, the front door opened. Adolpho walked in and was taken aback by the man sitting in their living room.

"Who are you?" Adolpho asked in Spanish, setting his paper on a table by the door.

"*¿Hablas ingles?*" Dmitri again asked.

"Reasonably well," Adolpho returned.

"My name is Dmitri. You and I were in school together for a short time. Do you remember?" Dmitri said, sipping from his teacup.

"Do you remember Dmitri?" Adolpho's mother asked in her native tongue.

"No, mother, I don't think I do. You say we were in school together?" Adolpho asked again to clarify.

"Yes, but I moved before we really got to know each other. It was so many years ago. It isn't surprising you don't remember. I was looking for another mutual friend, perhaps you recall him—his name is Sage?" Dmitri asked in a deliberate, monotone voice.

Adolpho's face went pale. His mother noticed the sudden change and asked after him.

"I'm fine, mother," Adolpho answered, regaining his composure. "I'm sorry, but I don't remember Sage, either," Adolpho said, hoping he'd masked his initial nonverbal response.

"Perhaps if I jog your memory," Dmitri started.

"I believe his family's business supplied parts for the Space Station, and that same company later manufactured very powerful video cards. Didn't you keep in touch?" Dmitri asked, knowing Adolpho couldn't ignore the coded message.

"Perhaps I do remember a "Sage," but I didn't know him well. I was planning to visit our local market. Dmitri, would you care to take a walk?" Adolpho asked, noting his mother had detected the awkward nature of the conversation.

"You just returned, son. Don't you want some breakfast before you go?"

"We won't be gone long, mother. Come, Dmitri. Let me show you a bit of Arocena," Adolpho said, walking toward the door.

When their feet touched the stone of the street, Adolpho immediately questioned Dmitri.

"Who are you?"

"I have spoken my given name, 'Dmitri,'" he answered coyly.

"Why have you come here?"

"I represent a group of gentlemen who are very interested in a game called 'Antiquity.' They have a plan, which, if executed properly, will yield great wealth. They will pay a king's wage to gain access to the game. Do you know the game—'Antiquity'?" Dmitri asked.

"Money has never interested me. My ideals, my causes, drive me," Adolpho said arrogantly, not answering Dmitri's question.

"Money can make ideals a reality. Money can buy revenge. Money can be the genesis of a cause. If you continue to use your turns carelessly, the others will combine their turns to alter all you mean to accomplish. Do you not see this?" Dmitri bluntly stated.

They continued their walk toward the town's market district without speaking. Vendors were busy setting up their stalls. It was an active, colorful place, but neither of the men were mindful of the surroundings.

"What would be required?"

"You would travel with me to our technology center. There, we are developing scenarios designed to generate a fortune. When successful, you would be paid . . . paid very well," Dmitri said, knowing the hook had been set.

"What would stop you from exploiting me? You could leave me penniless or worse," Adolpho pressed.

"You are wise to ask this. Using Antiquity turns is only part of the equation. We are also interested in a long-term relationship. New players will emerge. You can help us discover who they are and cultivate them. If you consent, I will have two million dollars deposited in your choice of accounts. This is a down payment. If our plans are not completely successful, this money is yours to keep, but I assure you, we will be successful, and you will earn tenfold this initial payment. You will be able to further any cause you wish."

Adolpho stopped walking. Dmitri stopped two steps ahead and turned.

"Problem?" Dmitri asked.

"When you prove what you have said, I will go with you. When we return to my home, I will give you the account numbers. I will be ready to travel when I see the transactions," he said, beginning to walk again.

"Fine, but we want assurances, too. I want to see you launch Antiquity and utilize the password that comes to mind. You must know that, if you should try to depart after receiving the funds, we will pursue you with extreme prejudice. Your mother will be the first target and . . . well, let's just say your mother's last days would be exceedingly painful. I find it regrettable that I must explain this, but it is important to understand the ramifications of poor decision-making," Dmitri said, stopping Adolpho from walking further by blocking his path.

"I prefer directness. I will honor our arrangement," Adolpho said, meeting Dmitri's stare.

"Very well. I am pleased you've chosen to work with us. Now, where is this market? My appetite is improving, and I believe your dear mother knows how to prepare an exceptional meal," Dmitri said, stepping aside to let Adolpho pass.

Dmitri was satisfied Adolpho was Sage after watching him bring Antiquity to life and enter the required password. As Dmitri suspected, Adolpho's mother was an excellent cook and prepared a delightful Mediterranean dinner boasting fresh seafood and all the trimmings. Dmitri left the Delgado residence with a full stomach and a feeling of accomplishment.

In two days' time, the promised two million was distributed into the half-a-dozen accounts Adolpho had specified. Spreading the deposits avoided the scrutiny of having such a large sum hitting only one account. In addition to the funds, an airline ticket, final destination Russia, was delivered. Adolpho was in a joyous mood the morning he left for the airport. He gave his mother an unusually healthy sum to tide her over until his return and then kissed her goodbye. Sage was already planning revenge against the other players who had conspired to interfere with his previous efforts. He knew the wealth soon to be his would make all things possible. Patience and careful planning were the only requirements.

Adolpho's flight was uneventful. The plane landed in Moscow as the evening sun fell to the horizon. He wondered for a moment what the passengers on the flight he'd doomed must have felt as they plummeted to the ground, but he didn't dwell there long. Adolpho was firm in his conviction that this was a necessary step, regardless of the cost in flesh. Now was the time to be forward-thinking. He was a member of a new partnership and felt a sense of importance he had never experienced. Adolpho was met by a man who helped with his luggage and who opened the SUV's door to allow entrance. This further boosted his ego. *A man of importance should be treated so,* he thought as he nodded his approval before taking a seat.

Driving through Moscow, Adolpho looked with fascination at the famous landmarks he had seen in schoolbooks—the Kremlin, Red Square, St. Basil's Cathedral. Thinking back to his early years, he never envisioned he would step foot in this country, and now he was entering it on a red carpet. The driver made his way through the picturesque city without speaking, allowing Adolpho to take things in with no distraction. As the kilometers accumulated, the city became smaller, and Adolpho leaned back and closed his eyes. Adolpho estimated they had traveled twenty kilometers or more since leaving the city limits. He opened his eyes when the car slowed and watched as they entered a compound that looked more military than high-tech. Chain-link fencing adorned with razor wire stretched a block in each direction. The driver pulled to a stop at a guardhouse, where a man in fatigues requested ID before making a call. Adolpho thought he would be driven to a gleaming glass tower, not an encampment. Passing through the gate, the SUV traveled the snow-covered road to the front of the principal building. The extreme cold astonished Adolpho, and he felt fortunate that they were but a few meters from the entrance.

Another security check awaited in a lobby surrounded by foreboding architecture that smacked of the repressive days when the country had gone by a different name. Adolpho stood imagining what these walls had seen. In short order, Dmitri rounded the corner at the far end of the hall and walked at a deliberate pace toward them.

"Adolpho, welcome to Russia, and welcome to our technology center. It may not look like Silicon Valley, but I assure you, our technology and our talent rival the world's best. Was your flight a pleasant one?" Dmitri asked, giving Adolpho time to respond.

"The flight went well, and I enjoyed the ride from the city. Moscow was more impressive than I expected," Adolpho answered, holding comment on the quality of the tech until he could judge for himself.

"Come; let me show you to your room. Although you may find the building's stance imposing, I believe you will find the accommodations very comfortable," Dmitri said, picking up one of Adolpho's bags.

Adolpho's face registered the concerns occupying his mind. The facility was completely different from his original vision. Adolpho remained silent as they walked the wide corridors.

Dmitri pulled a small envelope from his breast pocket and removed a plastic card. As was common in most modern hotels, he waved the card by the latch, and the door's lock softly pinged. Dmitri opened the door. The room was as promised—well-appointed with luxurious linens, subdued color tones, beautiful paintings, and granite surfaces that shone light blue when viewed at an angle.

Adolpho's mood was instantly transformed.

"This is an amazing room. The paintings . . . original?" he asked as he set his bag on the floor beside the bed.

"Of course. We attract the best talent by paying well and providing unrivaled comfort. We work hard, but we enjoy ourselves," Dmitri said, smiling. "Please refresh yourself, and I will return to take you to dinner in thirty minutes."

Dmitri tossed the key cards on the bed and let himself out.

As announced, Dmitri returned to escort Adolpho to dinner. With Adolpho's revived outlook, he found it easy to talk as they walked. Dmitri stopped before a set of gold-metallic elevator doors. When the car arrived, they stepped in, and Dmitri selected the floor two levels below. When they stepped off the elevator, their senses were bombarded with aromas that were savory, smoky, and sweet. They passed a large vase of fresh-cut flowers as they entered the main dining room. *This is how one should live,* Adolpho thought as the maître d' escorted them to a table. The room was full of people, but only low murmurs were audible. Adolpho attributed this to the many plush draperies and soft floor coverings.

"Do all your employees live here? Are they permitted to leave?"

"This is no prison. We go to town, we shop, we play, we live, but, as I said, we are driven, and we work intently to achieve our goals," Dmitri said as the waiter stepped tableside.

They ordered and drank wine, and generally enjoyed themselves. Adolpho thought about life after the promised wealth was his. He would first serve retribution upon the high school children who had thwarted his efforts. Once complete, he would build a great house and fill it with all the trappings men of his stature deserved. He would care for his mother and work to free those oppressed by attacking the Western pigs controlling the world. Sage went to sleep with visions of a future he never dreamt possible.

The next morning, Adolpho found his way to the dining room and ordered sausages, pastry, and coffee. On the way back, he crossed paths with Dmitri.

"Are you ready to work, Adolpho?"

"Yes, I'm eager to begin."

"Let me show you the way," Dmitri said, pointing back toward the elevator.

"Will I need my computer?" Adolpho asked, taking a step back toward his room.

"Not today. I first want to explain our approach. Once we are certain we have a scenario which will maximize our profit, you will use a turn," Dmitri said as he beckoned Adolpho to follow.

Dimitri escorted Adolpho to a roomful of neatly arranged cubicles and office chairs. The room's lighting was subdued but provided the level of brightness required at each workstation. Multiple screens sat on each desk. Displayed on the screens were graphs, spreadsheets, and windows of what appeared to be source code. Dmitri led Adolpho to a conference room lined with whiteboards. He invited Adolpho to sit, after which Dmitri cleaned one of the boards, picked up a marker, and began to draw. Dmitri explained that his employers had many worldwide ventures, all being administered from this building. He drew multiple blocks representing shell companies. Each shell company had many holdings of stocks and commodities. Dmitri continued by drawing several graphs beside the blocks. He pointed to the people on the other side of the glass-walled conference room and said that they were analyzing scenarios aimed at maximizing profit if the world's markets could be manipulated. They were looking for a specific moment when the holdings in each of these companies could be traded ahead of an event no one else knew was coming. Initial models showed a profit of several billion dollars could be reaped if the plan succeeded. When the teams agreed on a scenario, Antiquity would be used to shift the event to a known time. The teams would then execute preloaded trade orders.

Adolpho was extremely impressed with the plan. "I didn't know Antiquity could be used in this way."

"It has been done before but not on this scale. The beauty is that only a few people inhabiting this planet will realize it happened. There are so many companies, and the trades will be completely legal. No agency will have grounds to investigate," Dmitri said with a slight nod.

"Won't the high school children use their turns to reverse what you've done?" Adolpho asked with concern.

"We don't think so. We believe they will hold onto their turns for fear they will be needed to reverse some future catastrophe. We can thank you for that," Dmitri said, implying that Sage's tendency toward violence had paved an advantageous path.

"I did what I did for the world's oppressed people," Adolpho said defiantly.

"Yes, I understand, but it had an unintended consequence, one that benefits us. I'm grateful," Dmitri said, patting Adolpho on the shoulder.

Adolpho relaxed. By day's end, he was on-board and ready to play his part. After a great deal of research, the team was nearing the end of their work. By the fourth day of Adolpho's arrival, they had converged on a solution—a volatile day of trading that matched the criteria they were seeking. If this day could be shifted into their present, they could make trades and net an estimated two and a half billion dollars, U.S.

The team made their pitch to Aleksei and the company's principals. After weighing everything presented, it was agreed that this was the chance they'd been hunting. Aleksei turned his gaze to Adolpho, and the rest of the room followed suit. Adolpho stood and announced he was ready. Aleksei slowly clapped his hands, the room following his lead.

Dmitri assured him that the trade orders had been programmed ahead of time. He and Adolpho would be the only two people in the building who would be aware of the changes. Adolpho now sat in front of his computer. Antiquity's images danced across the screen. Adolpho entered the password and typed his request as Dmitri watched.

Delay February 3rd's worldwide market and commodity trades until February 27th.

"Are you sure this will work? None of us, me or the other players, ever tried changing history in this way," Adolpho stated, hesitating to send the request.

"Yes. Have confidence, Adolpho. I have seen this before; it will work. Please proceed," Dmitri said, pointing at the "Enter" key.

Adolpho did as he was asked.

Your event is being administered. You will be notified when complete.

It was the evening of February 26th. A special meal was ordered by Aleksei. All ate well and drank heavily.

When Adolpho returned to his room, he stumbled, bumping against the side of his bed, having had more wine than was prudent. He fell onto the down-filled comforter that lay on his bed and felt a slight spinning sensation. Pulling a pillow under his head, he attempted to gain control of his mind and body. His computer was to his left; he reached for it and raised the top. The alcohol affected his ability to sense the password floating in his mind. It took three attempts before he was successful. He stared at the five words centered on his screen.

Your event change is complete.

He let his head fall back against the pillow. *Tomorrow would be a day like no other.* He closed his eyes and didn't move again until morning was well underway.

Adolpho's mouth was dry and pasty. He swung his legs over the edge of the bed and rubbed his face. Getting to his feet, he walked to the bathroom sink and filled his cup three times, trying to rehydrate. He turned on the shower and crawled in. The warm water helped him to get his bearings. In thirty-five minutes, he was walking to the dining room in a quest for caffeine. He met Dmitri in the dining room and joined him.

"I'm feeling the effects of last night," Adolpho said, taking a gulp of coffee.

"I, too, enjoyed in excess, but my adrenaline is winning. I am anxious for the day to begin."

Neither of them ate, choosing instead to rely on their coffee for sustenance. When they were finished, they walked to the computer room and met the rest of last night's revelers. Everyone in the room looked hungover, but they were at their desks watching the trading patterns. They seemed puzzled. They weren't expecting the volatility they were seeing.

"They don't remember," Dmitri said. "They don't realize they are living through February 3rd's trading day."

"We have buy/sell orders scheduled. Who authorized them?" one of the employees asked in a manner that grabbed everyone's attention.

"I did," Dmitri said firmly. "Everything should be allowed to execute as is—do you understand? Do not alter anything."

All was occurring as planned. By sunset, their profits exceeded their estimate. They had increased the wealth of the enterprise by two and three quarter billion dollars. It was an incredible success. In three days' time, twenty million dollars was deposited in Adolpho's Swiss account in payment for his participation. He promised to cooperate on future endeavors, but, for now, he said he wanted to return home to care for his mother.

When he arrived home, he called the man he'd hired to find Jeffery.

"I want to schedule a trip, and I will need your help," Adolpho began. "Money is no impediment," Adolpho continued. "Yes, I will need a passport under a new name. It must be clean. Where? The United States, for a vacation. Don't ask why; just provide what I am asking. I will also need you to arrange for a weapon to be made available—a pistol. I told you money is not a problem. Yes . . . yes, very good." Adolpho finished and tossed the phone onto his bed.

"I told them they would regret their actions," he proudly articulated as he walked to the kitchen.

CHAPTER 46

WE SAW ANTIQUITY'S NOTICE ARRIVE ON-SCREEN. Tatiana and I wondered if we should use a turn to reverse Sage's effort and called Catherine to ask her advice.

Catherine said it was important to save our turns for extremely serious situations, like the Space Station—or worse. She agreed that manipulating markets wasn't ethical but said that it was not worth burning turns. She also said we needed to think ahead. Sage wasn't the only danger. Antiquity would appear again, and there would be more players. Every turn could become critical. A turn could stop a world war. Besides, she mentioned, even with the short notice, our previous players helped our government and several senators take partial advantage.

"It looks like everyone is happy with Sage's use of a turn," I said, rolling my eyes as I told Tatiana. "Several of our distinguished citizens made money off of Sage. It never ends," I said as we walked to the mess hall.

"America isn't perfect," Tatiana said, laughing at me. "At least you try to make things legitimate. In Russia, they don't even try anymore."

"Do you know what Catherine meant by 'help us through high school'? Does she mean we need to move to Washington? I didn't think about this when she was talking."

"I don't know. We should ask," Tatiana said as she drank her sweet iced tea. "I like this cold tea."

I laughed, and we walked in the direction of our rooms.

When we arrived at Tatiana's room, I greeted Alena and Mrs. Smirnov. It was nice to see Tatiana's mom doing better. After saying our goodnights, Tatiana stepped outside the room with me and closed the door. I said a quiet "Goodnight" and slowly turned toward my room. Looking back, I saw she hadn't reached to open the door. I stopped and stepped back to where she was standing, put my hand on her waist, pulled her to me, and kissed her. I felt a rush of adrenaline as my lips touched hers. They were soft and full, and I tasted a subtle sweet saltiness. As I slowly pulled away, she put her hand on the side of my face, and we kissed again.

"Goodnight, Jeffery," she whispered with her sweet accent.

"Goodnight," I said, letting go of her hand. I waited until she entered her room.

When I got back to my room, mom and dad were there, and I figured I'd better tell them what Catherine wanted.

"Well, honey, I am so proud of you, and what she is offering is an honor. But is she talking about you moving to Washington? Don't you think you should finish high school back home? How could you possibly transfer now?"

mom asked as her mind whirled through every scenario under the sun.

"I know. I'm not sure what she means. But college sounds like it could be something. I like the people I've met—the CIA people who saved me, Tatiana, and her family. They put their lives out there for us," I said, with a passion I hadn't previously felt. Mom and dad were looking at each other like I wasn't their son.

"I've never heard you talk like this, except about computer games," dad said, trying to lighten things up.

"I'm serious, dad," I replied.

"Can we sit down together to talk to Catherine?" mom asked, sounding calmer than a minute ago.

"I'm good with that, but I want Tatiana there and her family, too, if they want."

Mom and dad looked at each other and nodded.

"I'm calling Catherine," I said, picking up my phone.

By the time I hung up, we had an appointment for the following morning at nine-thirty.

"Sorry I was so intense."

"It's okay. It's nice to hear you fired up about something this important," dad answered.

"I'll be back . . . I've got to tell Tatiana."

"You could call her," mom said.

"That's okay. I feel like walking."

Mom and dad looked at each other and smiled.

Tatiana was watching American TV, as she called it, with her mom and sister. She joined me in the hall, and I told her about the appointment and what I'd told mom and dad. I let her know she could bring her mom and Alena along. She thanked me but said she thought it better if she heard what Catherine had to say first; then she would tell her mom and sister in her own words.

———❈———

We met, as planned, with Catherine the next morning. She clarified things. When she'd said, "help us through high school," she meant she would offer protection to keep our Russian "friends" from getting to us or our families. Her offer to help us through college was amazing. Full scholarships, room, board, books, you name it, at one of five top schools. The condition: work for the CIA for four years after graduation. We said we wanted to think about it, but I knew this was what I wanted to do. Tatiana wasn't letting on, but I had a feeling that she felt the same. Maybe we were becoming adrenaline junkies. Something changed because of our adventure, and I knew there was no going back to my old ways. We talked it over with our families, and, in neither case were they able to change our teenage minds. By that night, we both called Catherine and accepted.

Two days later, we were driving home. I was thinking about school. I mean, high school, compared to all we'd been through, was going to feel like kindergarten. Compared with Tatiana and her sister, I had it easy. For them, a new country, a new school, a new home, a new group of people—new everything—they had to be stressing big time.

We called Yoko during the ride. She was so happy that we were free, and she thanked us a hundred times for using Antiquity to save them. Her mom and dad didn't remember anything, but Yoko did and described the torture her mom had endured. Catherine called her and made an incredible offer to send her to college, but she wasn't sure it was right. Yoko's response to all that had happened was the opposite of ours; she wanted less, not more. She wanted to settle into the life she knew before Antiquity. She was appreciative for all the U.S. government was doing to take care of her family but didn't have a desire to come to the United States. I wanted her to come, but I didn't try to persuade her. It was a huge decision, and it was hers to make.

We pulled into our drive a few hours later. I stood beside the rented SUV and stretched, trying to loosen up.

"I like your home, Jeffery," Tatiana said, pointing at the flower boxes hanging by the windows. "They must be beautiful in summer."

"I like it, too," I said as I looked at her, thinking how unreal it all was.

Thanks to mom, the guest rooms were neat, clean, and inviting. She always did things right. Mom and dad had finished the basement, so grandma could come and live with us, but she passed before she spent a night. It wasn't five-star, but there were a couple of bedrooms, a bathroom, and a small kitchen. It would do until Tatiana and her family could find their own place. For me, I hoped it would take a while.

Catherine and her CIA crowd arranged for the visas and the required paperwork to get Tatiana and Alena enrolled in school, and they went so far as to hook Mrs. Smirnov up with some Russians who lived close to us. *Tatiana and her family may not stay Stateside in the long run,* I thought, *but everyone was trying to make things work.*

It was Friday. We had the weekend before we had to deal with school. We drove the Smirnovs around and spent time chillin' on the sofa, watching movies. It was awesome, and I didn't want it to end. But Monday showed up, and I helped Tatiana and Alena get their start. I gave them the grand tour and introduced them to friends. I felt like I was abandoning them when I walked to class, but as time passed, we got into a rhythm. They were making friends, and both Alena and Tatiana were brilliant, showing they could compete with anyone. All was going better than expected.

Sage passed through customs without incident. His newly acquired name was Felipe Aquino. Homeland Security would see a model citizen, so well-constructed were his documents. Key databases had been carefully altered, so there would be no gaps to raise suspicion.

Felipe was staying at the Ritz Carlton. His "vacation" was proceeding as planned, and he was enjoying his stay with the "Capitalist pigs." Having never been in the United States, let alone New York, he found the hustle and bustle of the city energizing. New York was amazing, especially when one was traveling with abundant resources. He ate heartily and spent substantial sums, buying clothes and gifts, which he shipped home. Felipe was living large, but the reason for his stay in America was never far from his mind. He purchased tickets for the train to DC, arranged for a rental car, and reserved a room at a local B&B. A small tactical shop on the outskirts of DC would have a handgun and ammunition ready for pickup. It was time for Filipe's alter ego Sage to take center stage, and he prepared himself on his drive to Lexington. The next task: to get to know the area and study the patterns of his quarry. Aware that Jeffery and Tatiana could have people protecting them, he needed to take great care. Casing Jeffery's neighborhood over the course of several days, he noted a car occupied by two men no more than four hundred meters from Jeffery and Tatiana. He also suspected there were others watching their families. The Americans knew the value of Antiquity and those able to use it. Sage would take as long as necessary to see things properly attended.

Sage continued to gather intelligence but was careful to obscure his efforts. He rented a second car to alternate between days. He hired Uber drivers and took cabs. He took walks around the school and the neighborhood. Piece by piece, he was building a detailed report of the composition of Jeffery and Tatiana's lives. When he felt his reconnoitering was finished, he went back to his hotel, the fourth residence he had taken since arriving in the area. He laid his notes end to end and commenced his search for windows of opportunity.

There were three locations along Jeffery and Tatiana's walk home from school where the topography created blind spots. He estimated the duration they were hidden from view was twenty-five, fifteen, and forty-five seconds, respectively. The first was reasonable, but the last provided the lowest risk. Another benefit in choosing the latter location was a side road which allowed for exit without exposure to the agents guarding the pair. Sage realized he would need a method to get them into a vehicle without incident. He would once again contact his Spanish friend, who had been so instrumental in finding Jeffery initially, and request CIA identification. If he played it properly, Jeffery and Tatiana would believe a threat had been detected. Once in the car, Sage would guide them to a second location, chosen for its relative isolation. Moments later, his business would be attended to, and he would drive away in a second car staged in advance.

He rehearsed the plan again and again to ensure his execution would be without flaw. He drove the intended route several times to familiarize himself with the traffic patterns and to get a sense of timing. His identification arrived on Wednesday, and it was an impressive piece of work. He laughed when he considered that, on paper, he was now aligned with the CIA. It was ironic to think he would use the credentials of an organization that stood for everything he hated. *Friday will be the day*, he thought. *Friday they will see my eyes, and they will know.*

We set out for school Friday morning as we had every school day since Tatiana had joined our family. Alena's English was improving steadily, and it was fun to talk to her. Before, our conversations were composed of a few words and mostly concerned Antiquity, so I didn't know her, but I learned she had a great sense of humor. We laughed and talked about our teachers on the way—the good ones and those who had chosen the wrong occupation. Alena and

Tatiana said it was the same in Russia. I noticed our security guys as we walked by. That must be boring . . . mostly sitting and watching.

We'd walked on another five hundred feet or so, when a car skidded to a stop a few yards ahead.

"Quickly! I need to get you to safety. We have a credible threat. A Russian gang intends to abduct you," said a man holding his ID so that we could see it. "Get in. Jeffery, you drive. I may need both hands," he said, waving us toward the car.

We looked at each other for a moment before running to the car.

"Which way?" I asked, shifting the car into "Drive."

"Down this side road," the CIA man said, pointing.

I followed his instructions as we sped away. He continued to direct me and said that we were to meet another CIA team who would take us to a safe house. We had no reason to doubt. He had an accent, but we knew the CIA hired people from every corner of the world.

After fifteen miles, we were traveling a road more stone and grass than pavement.

"There's the car, just ahead. Do you see? Stop there," he said urgently.

I pulled to a stop behind the parked car.

"Everyone out—quickly," he said loudly.

We piled out of the car. Something didn't seem right. Where was the team that was to take us to safety? We were standing by the parked car—the CIA agent was looking left and right.

"The team, they should be here," he said in a convincing tone. "Something must be wrong," he said as I saw him pull his pistol. He looked side to side once more, and his movements suddenly slowed. His mode shifted from urgent and edgy to an out-of-place calm. He turned his head and looked at us.

"I once told you I would seek retribution," he said coldly.

Tatiana, Alena, and I looked at each other.

"I don't understand," I replied, confused, my heart rate rising.

"You . . . you and the others, you should have let my plan for the Space Station unfold as intended. The war would have ended centuries of exploitation. After it was over, a new world would have been born," he spouted, as if quoting the beginning lines of a manifesto.

"Sage, that's not the way. This isn't the way," I said, hoping for some consideration.

"Violence is the only avenue for great change, and it would have been a beautiful war. When you are dead, only your Japanese friend will remain. She will be next. Then I will use my final turn to complete what I started," he said as he raised his pistol and pointed it at Tatiana.

I shifted to block his view of Tatiana and Alena.

"You first, brave one," he laughed as he walked closer, straightening his arm to improve his aim.

I reached back for Tatiana's hand. I wanted her touch to be the last thing I felt. Sage was at my side. He jammed the muzzle against my head. A small stream of blood ran down the front of my forehead and into my right eye. "Antiquity will not help you this time. I will take care of your Japanese comrade before she can determine what's happened. There will be no one left to play," he said as his laugh faded.

I could feel the mechanisms of the pistol engaging through the metal pressed to my head. Sage seemed to be enjoying the moment, prolonging it at my expense. I closed both eyes, readying myself for the bullet's impact.

My body flinched as a shot rang out. The gun pressed against my head jerked and scraped across my face. I opened my eyes and saw Sage lying motionless on the ground at my feet. The right side of his head was gone, and blood was flowing from his shattered skull, coloring the grass just beginning to show the green of early spring. It was a grotesque scene. We had seen our share of death and blood over the last weeks, but this was as bad as any. None of us could make sense of what had happened.

We turned when we heard the sound of footsteps to our left. Two men, one carrying a sniper's rifle, the other a set of high-power binoculars, emerged.

"Y'all alright?" the man with the binoculars asked.

None of us answered his question.

"I doubt you know who to trust right now. We caught wind of this guy making his rounds at your school, so we started following him. He was pretty good at covering his tracks. We didn't know what he was up to or who he was. Damn good thing we were keeping an eye on things, as it turns out. I'm sorry, guys. I hear y'all have been through a lot. We have people on the way. This guy can't hurt you anymore," he said as he lit a cigarette.

In fifteen minutes, twenty vehicles arrived, lights flashing. I called Catherine to let her know what was going down. She said she'd already been briefed and was on her way. I felt I could trust Catherine. She didn't have a big personality, but she'd followed through on everything she'd promised, at least so far.

We sat in Catherine's car for an hour or so, talking about Sage. Catherine said they'd been focusing their efforts on the Russian mobs. They weren't expecting Sage to pull this. She gave us a ride back home and said she thought it best if we didn't discuss this with anyone outside of family or the agency. I think I spoke for all of us when I told her we didn't want to talk about it anyway.

Mom and dad opened the door as we neared the front of my house. Catherine had called them after I had called her. Catherine didn't pull away until she saw us step inside. We sat in the family room and shared only a word or two, "Are you hungry? Can I get you anything?" We replied, "No, thanks." I knew Tatiana and Alena were having the same problem I was—shaking the image of Sage, his body lying in that awkward position and all that blood.

<hr>

Life settled down after all that insanity. The picture in our heads faded with time. Tatiana and her family moved into an apartment not far from the house, and Tatiana and I graduated high school that spring. Alena would be a senior the following year. That summer, we prepared for the start of our college days and hung out at the pool when we got the chance. Tatiana and I decided to attend the same university, and Catherine once again followed through on all her commitments. Her staff members pushed through our applications, and they helped with all aspects of getting set up for fall semester.

College was a tough go, but we worked our tails off and did well. Along with our parents, Catherine attended graduation. She was genuinely proud of us. Alena went on to be a veterinarian. She was always reaching out to help some creature in need, so her vocation was a perfect choice. Mrs. Smirnov met a cool Russian guy, and they got along like the two peas in that pod mom and dad always talked about.

We lost our lovely Yoko, not to a nefarious party of Russians, but by her own hand. Yoko took her life on the eve of her twenty-first birthday. I will never forget the day when I answered the phone and was given the news. Tatiana and I had grown close to Yoko, not in a geographic respect, but through calls, emails, and texts. We felt we knew her well. She was incredible. She was at the top of her class in college, she volunteered regularly at the children's ward, and she had a huge heart. Tatiana and I never sensed the pain overwhelming her. I've never completely forgiven myself for that. Yoko left a note on the table beside the empty prescription bottle; in the note, she emphatically expressed Antiquity not be used to change what she had done. She said further that she'd never felt completely comfortable in this world, that she didn't belong here. I wanted to tell her the world was a diminished place now that she was gone. Though she didn't understand her place in the world, the world needed her. Tatiana and I flew to Japan for her funeral and prayed with her parents. They were beyond devastated. They, too, felt the guilt of thinking there was something more they should have done. I guess there will always be more than one victim with a suicide. We said what we could to let them know what a special woman Yoko was, but there were no words able to cure or explain what had gone wrong. In the years following Yoko's death, Tatiana and I were devoted volunteers at the suicide-prevention center in town. We wanted to do all we could to prevent another beautiful soul leaving prematurely.

Tatiana and I still work for the agency. I never had occasion to use the last of my turns, but that may change soon. There are four new players now, and indications are two of them are drunk with the power Antiquity has given them. Our hope is that good will win out, but we are certain Dmitri and his band will seek advantage. Perhaps the remaining two players will unite as we once did. Time will tell.

It's time to put down my laptop. I see my lovely daughter running toward me calling my new name—"Daddy." My beautiful Tatiana isn't far behind. I guess I didn't say this: Yeah, she did feel the same way I did. We've had to work through some tough stuff. The scars left by her father's abandonment still burn from time to time, but she now has faith that there are a few good guys out there. Hell, she married me, and I take that as a compliment. And our first miracle, our daughter, who goes by the name of Yasmine Yoko McGregor, will soon have a baby sister to play with.

I don't believe the agency will ever let me publish these ramblings, and, even if they did, it would sit on a shelf in the fiction section—who would believe a word of it?